FEATHER TONGUE

Elowen Greywell

Published by Hillsather Publishing House www.elowengreywell.

com

Curated and edited by Callum Ward, Junior Editor & Archivist under the supervision of Benedict Lowre, Archivist Emeritus

ISBN: 979-8-9993361-5-6

Printed in the United States of America

Catalogued under: Literary Fiction, Gothic Horror, Archival Curiosities

To be managed with care. Contents may unsettle.

To the sweetest boy who never did live

The Montparnasse Times March 3rd, 1999

"A Prophet with a Pen": Young Author J.M. Errevale Stuns Religious World with Debut Novel

St. Luden's, Lozère, France—In a literary debut that critics are calling "divinely inspired," thirteen-year-old cloistered youth J.M. Errevale has captured national attention with the release of his first manuscript, *Where God Prays*. Written entirely from within the walls of the reclusive St. Luden's Chapel, the text is described by clergy and theologians alike as "miraculous," "visionary," and "beyond the reach of ordinary youth."

Little is known about the boy behind the words. Described by caretakers as "soft-spoken, radiant, and deeply devout," Errevale has lived under the care of the chapel since early childhood. He has reportedly never left the grounds.

The novel—woven with poetic scripture and mystical imagery—follows an abandoned monastery where God is rumoured to visit once a year to pray in solitude. The monks, forbidden to speak or approach, must live their entire lives preparing the house for a divine presence they are never permitted to witness. It is a meditation on absence, faith, and the unbearable weight of unseen holiness.

"Errevale's voice is not his own," said Father Bell of the Congregation for Sacred Writings. "It is the voice of something older. Something holy."

A second manuscript, sources say, is already underway—though no official title has been confirmed.

Pilgrims have already begun arriving at St. Luden's Chapel, hoping to catch a glimpse of the boy many are calling "the Sleeping Prophet."

Clémence Jouvet, Religious Correspondent

I warn everyone who hears the words of the prophecy of this book: if anyone adds to them, God will add to him the plagues described in this book, and if anyone takes away from the words of the book of this prophecy, God will take away his share in the tree of life and in the holy city.

Revelations 22:18-19

Cassette 001

[A faint click.]

[The tape hums, followed by a soft throat clear.]

I... I don't really know how to start one of these.

The sisters gave me this recorder. It was a... sort of gift, I think. For finishing the book. It was wrapped really neatly in paper, and Sister Carita even tied a bow from the old altar lace. I almost didn't want to open it. It felt like a present for someone else.

There was a note tucked underneath the bow. It just said, "For the gifted."

I didn't know how to feel about that.

They mean well. I think they always mean well. But sometimes the kindness feels... strange. Like a coat that doesn't quite fit, even if it's made of nice fabric...

[He clears his throat again.]

Anyway—this recorder.

I've never used one before. I didn't know they made this humming noise. It's like something's breathing just inside the casing. I keep thinking someone's going to knock on my door and tell me it's too loud, even though it isn't.

Father Bell says it might help me to talk things out. Out loud, I mean. That it's good for people "like me" to have some kind of outlet.

I asked what he meant by "like me," and he said, "Precocious. Devout. Brilliant, but quiet."

He smiled after that. I didn't.

I've been told I'm quiet a lot. It's not meant as an insult, I don't think, but it always feels like one. I just don't always have the right words when I need them. They come hours later, when it's too late to say anything. Or they pile up all at once and get stuck in my throat.

It's like trying to breathe through cloth.

Sometimes I hum, when I can't speak. Sister Marianne says she hears me doing it when I'm shelving books. I didn't realize. I think it's just something I do so I don't feel... I don't know. Alone? Or maybe like I'm still here.

There are a lot of moments I don't feel real. I don't mean that in a sad way. Just... like I'm watching myself from the rafters or behind the altar, and everyone else is moving normally while I'm a few seconds behind.

Maybe that's what writing is. Catching up.

[A pause.]

The book's done. Printed. Bound. Sent away to people with clean desks and expensive pens. I'm told I should be proud.

[He pauses again, taking a breath.]

I'm not unproud. I just don't feel anything about it. Or... not the right things. It's like it happened to someone else. A better version of me. The "gifted" one.

They say God spoke through me. That I've been given the gift of prophecy, or something of that nature. I don't hate it, who could hate being chosen by God? It's just a bit... strange sometimes.

When they ask what I'm writing next, I say I don't know. But I do. I always do. The next story always starts before I finish the last one— it just hides for a while.

Like... there's this boy I've been thinking about.

He's different. I don't know how yet, exactly. But he was born with wings inside him. Not big ones. Just... soft ones. Feathers where his voice should be.

He doesn't talk. Can't, really. But when he tries, something happens to the people around him. They forget things. Tiny things. Names. Colours. The sound of their mother's laugh. Or maybe big things. Like their reflections or friends or families.

And I don't think he means to do it. I think he just wants to be heard. But every time he opens his mouth, someone else loses a piece of themselves.

So he stays quiet.

I think... I think he scares himself.

I know that's silly. It's just a story. But I keep thinking about him. About how lonely that must be. How it must feel to be afraid of your own voice.

Maybe I'm writing about him because I feel a little like that sometimes.

Like I take up too much space just by existing. Or like the things I say might ruin something I didn't mean to touch.

There are days where I don't say anything out loud. Not one word. And no one notices. Or maybe they do and just don't mention it.

The chapel is good for that. It's full of quiet places where you can disappear without really going anywhere.

There's a room behind the east transept that no one uses anymore. It smells like dust and old violets. I sit there sometimes after evening prayers. Not to pray. Just to sit.

There's a stained-glass window of Saint Michael with a sword drawn. He looks angry. Like he knows something we don't and doesn't have time to explain it.

I don't think angels should be angry.

I think they should be sad.

That's how I picture them, anyway. Not warriors. Just… tired.

Maybe that's how the boy feels, too. The one in my story. Not cursed. Not dangerous. Just exhausted from being made different.

Sometimes I wonder if the nuns and the priest see me like that. Not really a boy. Just a… thing that writes. A mouthpiece. A symbol of God.

When people call me gifted, they usually mean "useful."

And when they call me quiet, I think they mean "manageable."

I don't think I'm ungrateful. I like living here. I like the bells, and the gardens, and the way the library smells like candle wax and fruity polish.

But I don't think I've ever belonged anywhere. Not really.

Maybe that's what the story's about. Belonging. Or what happens when someone never learns how to.

I'm not sure how it ends yet.

Maybe the boy forgets his own voice, like everyone else. Or maybe he learns how to sing without hurting anyone.

Maybe that's all we're trying to do, really. Find a way to speak that doesn't take anything from anyone.

[He pauses again. An audible breath held for a long time.]

This was longer than I meant it to be.

If you're listening to this—well, I guess I mean me. If I'm listening to this later... I hope I still remember what it felt like to talk like this.

Just to say things without fixing them first. Without checking if they sound holy.

I think that's all I wanted. Just to try being a person again, instead of a voice.

[Faint clatter—the sound of the recorder being shifted. His voice returns softer, almost hesitant to end.]

I know I don't really have to say everything out loud.

But maybe it's easier this way. When I write, I start to sound like someone else. Like I'm trying to impress God. Or the priests. Or some reviewer with velvet gloves and a fancy oak wood desk.

Talking like this feels… different. Like I'm just a boy again. Not the one doing interviews for the papers. Not the one they keep calling "miraculous."

Just me. A little too small for my age. Sitting on the edge of my cot with cold feet and too many thoughts.

I wonder if it's wrong to feel afraid of the thing that makes you special.

Or if it's normal.

Maybe everyone feels that way, deep down. Like they're carrying something they didn't ask for and don't know how to name.

I hope the boy in the story finds someone who understands him. Who doesn't try to fix him, or worship him, or call him cursed.

Just someone who listens when he opens his mouth—even if no sound comes out.

[A quiet breath.]

Maybe that's what the recorder's for.

Maybe it can listen, even when no one else does.

[A long pause.]

[A small click. Then—very faintly—he hums a few off-key notes, unsure, seemingly half-lost in thought.]

[Click.]

I

I

The chapel seemed to breathe.

It did not move as living things do, but rather, expanded.

Slowly.

Reverently.

With each gust of cold air pushed through its long and broken windows. Dust spun through the and the stones themselves seemed to settle deeper into their foundations with each passing hour.

Beyond the walls, the countryside had gone to rot. Autumn had arrived early that year, stripping the trees bare before their time, leaving the earth raw and exposed. Wind pressed against the stained glass, rattling the lead came that held Saint Michael's sword, blurring the blue of the Virgin's robes until she looked more like a drowning woman than a queen of heaven.

And in the hollow where the pews once stood, a woman was dying.

The sisters had prepared her for it. They had stripped the altar of its candles three days prior, when her screaming stopped and the silence began.

They had drained the water fonts, blessed each empty basin, and laid clean linen across the stone where her back now arched in ways that defied the architecture of spine and rib. The linen was already stained—not with blood, as one might expect, but with something darker. Something that smelled of copper and crushed violets and the wet interior of a birds' nests.

She did not scream, though something inside her had begun to tear.

Her name was Marguette, and she was too young to be dying this way.

Sister Bernadine had found her six months ago, collapsed in the herb garden among the feverfew and rosemary. At first, they thought she was a pilgrim—young women sometimes wandered to the chapel seeking sanctuary from unwanted marriages or pregnancies that bore too much shame. But Marguette had no belongings, no story, no memory of how she had arrived. She spoke only in fragments.

"The feathers hurt."

"It moves when I sleep."

"Something wants to be born."

No one knew how long she'd carried the child. Some said she had been born pregnant, that the baby had formed in her womb while she was still in her mother's belly—a nested pregnancy, a miracle of terrible biology.

Others whispered it had grown from a feather swallowed during Advent, that she had been eating communion bread when a dove moulted overhead, and the down had taken root in her throat before sliding down to bloom in her belly.

The most superstitious sisters claimed it had no father at all. That it had formed whole and trembling from the prayers pressed too long against her stomach, that divine longing had spontaneously generated flesh.

Sister Agatha, who served as the chapel's physician, had

examined her once. Only once. She emerged from the cell pale and shaking, clutching her rosary so tightly the beads left impressions in her palm.

"It's not a baby," she whispered to Mother Superior. "Not entirely."

When pressed for details, Sister Agatha would only say that the shape beneath Marguette's skin moved wrong. That it fluttered rather than kicked. That when she pressed her ear to the girl's belly, she heard not a heartbeat but something like wind through hollow bones.

Marguette had not spoken in days. Her lips were chapped with blood from where she bit them to keep from screaming. Her eyes rolled gently in her head as though following the flickering of wings that only she could see. Sometimes she would raise her hand to trace patterns in the air—figure eights, spirals, shapes that resembled letters in no alphabet the sisters recognized. Her fingertips left faint trails of light that lingered for just a moment before fading, though this might have been a trick of the candleflame.

The sisters worked in silence around her prone form, none daring to speak above the sounds her body made—the crack of bone expanding to accommodate something too large, the wet sound of skin giving way like overripe fruit, and underneath it all, the dry and paper-like rustle of feathers unfurling somewhere deep inside her chest cavity.

This was no birth the chapel had ever witnessed before.

It was quieter. Hungrier. More deliberate.

Sister Marie-Claire, who had attended seventeen deliveries in her forty years of service, said it felt less like midwifery and more like excavation. As though they were not helping something emerge, but uncovering something that had always been there, waiting beneath layers of flesh and blood and prayer.

The mother's ribs had spread. Not broken—that would have been merciful—but stretched, the cartilage elongating until her chest resembled the hull of an overturned boat. Her skin had bruised purple down the centre where something within pressed upward, toward her heart. Sister Agatha could trace the outline of it through the skin.

Not baby-shaped, but angular. Geometric. Like wings folded too tightly around a secret.

"The heart," Marguette whispered during one of her lucid moments. "It wants the heart."

The midwife, Sister Elene, had seen plenty of strange things in her sixty years. She had delivered babies born with cauls that bore the image of saints, twins who shared a single soul, a child who was born knowing Latin though her parents spoke only the local dialect. But this—this felt different. Ancient. Like something that had been trying to be born for centuries and had finally found the right vessel.

There were no screams. Only a thin, rasping noise as Marguette's throat opened, closed, and opened again. Like breathing, but wrong. Like her windpipe had become a bellows, drawing air not into her lungs but into some other cavity that shouldn't exist.

The contractions, when they came, were backwards. Instead of the rhythmic tightening that pushed downward, Marguette's body seemed to be pulling something up. Her stomach would concave, her ribs would flare, and she would arch her back until her spine formed a perfect C. During these episodes, the temperature in the chapel would drop by several degrees. Frost would form on the windows despite the season. The candles would flicker in unison, their flames bending toward her body as though drawn by an unseen wind.

Sister Bernadine began to pray the rosary, her voice steady

24

and low. The other sisters joined her, their Latin a protective wall of sound around the labouring woman. But even their prayers sounded strange in the changed air—hollow, echoing, as though the words were being swallowed before they could reach heaven.

When it came—when the child finally tore free—it did so without warning.

There was no final contraction, no push, no last plea for mercy or strength. There was just a sound. A sound like silk ripping. Like parchment tearing along a careful fold. Like lungs splitting at the seams.

And then...

Silence. Perfect, crystalline silence that rang in their ears like the aftermath of bells.

And the child.

It emerged not from below but from above, tearing through the skin of Marguette's chest in a spray of blood and amniotic fluid that smelled of myrrh and copper pennies. The wound it left behind was not jagged but precise, as though cut with surgical instruments. The edges were clean, almost ceremonial.

It was bloodied. Wrapped in mucus and feather-down that clung to its skin like wet snow. Its limbs were longer than they should have been, joints articulated in ways that suggested bird rather than human anatomy. Its mouth was sealed—fused shut as though the lips had grown together in the womb. Behind them, something coiled and ribboned: a tongue that was too long, too thin, covered in what looked like microscopic feathers that caught the candlelight and threw it back in tiny prisms.

Its eyes did not open, but its wings moved. Once. Just once.

They were not the vestigial wing-buds sometimes found on malformed infants, but actual wings. Small, yes, barely the span of a man's hand, but perfectly formed. Each feather was distinct, precise, coloured the pale grey of morning fog. When they moved, they scattered a fine layer of down across the linen, each piece of fluff settling like snow.

The mother was gone.

She had bled from her chest, not her womb, and her heart cavity had been emptied to make room. Not torn out, but rather absorbed. Consumed. Where her heart should have been, there was only a hollow space lined with the same pale feathers that covered the child. It was as though her heart had been traded, piece by piece, for whatever grew inside her.

Her face was peaceful. More peaceful than it had been in months. Her eyes were closed, her mouth slightly open in what might have been a smile. Sister Elene checked for breath, for pulse, for any sign of life, but found none. Marguette was as empty as a discarded cocoon.

The midwife, a woman named Sister Elene who had delivered half the children in three parishes, did not cry. She had learned long ago that some births were also deaths, that creation and destruction were often the same act viewed from different angles. She pressed the sign of the cross against the infant's feathered back, then wrapped him in still warm fabric of his mother's torn robe.

"Be not afraid," she whispered, more to herself than to the other sisters.

Sister Marie-Claire, who had been holding the holy water, asked if he was cursed.

Sister Elene did not answer immediately. She studied the child's face—the too-pale skin, the sealed mouth, the faint tracery of blue veins visible beneath the surface like a map of rivers. His breathing was so shallow as to be nearly imperceptible. His tiny chest rose and fell no more than a whisper.

"No," she said finally. "He will be listened to, but never heard."

The words came out before she fully understood what she meant by them. But once spoken, they felt true in a way that made her spine prickle. This child would never speak—but somehow, that would make him more powerful, not less. Silence, she realized, was not the absence of communication but a different language entirely.[1]

---

1   *"Should I be writing such depressing material?"*

II

The child was named Asael in the quiet, a name that seemed to encapsulate the divinity of his birth, as well as the blasphemy of it.

He was not baptized—Mother Superior declared that such ceremonies must wait until they better understood what they were dealing with. So in the days that followed, they did not write of his arrival.

There was no entry in the chapel registry, no announcement during vespers, no letter sent to the Bishop describing the miraculous birth. No. Asael's existence was as silent as himself. And almost as sacred.

He was only carried.

First to the sacristy, where the linen was rinsed of blood in three separate bowls (they would later discover that the blood would not wash clean, leaving permanent stains that resembled wing-shapes), then to the far west cell, where the sisters kept the reliquaries and relics too blasphemous to display.

The west cell was a narrow room with stone walls and a single window set high enough that only sky was visible through it. It had been used, in earlier centuries, to house sacred objects of questionable provenance—a vial of tears shed by Saint Lucia that glowed faintly in moonlight, a piece of cloth that was either from Christ's burial shroud or from the robe of a very clever forger, bones of saints whose sanctity was disputed by Rome but whose miracles were undeniably effective.

They laid him in a cot lined with wool and feather pulp. Sister Elene smoothed his brow with oil blessed during the previous Easter and stitched a small charm into the hem of his blanket: a wing and a thorn, embroidered in silk thread the colour of dried blood.

He did not cry.

This fact became more disturbing as the hours passed.[2] All babies cried—it was how they announced their arrival, how they filled their lungs with the breath of life. But this child remained silent, his small chest rising and falling in a rhythm so gentle it was barely perceptible. When Sister Bernadine leaned close to check if he was still breathing, she could hear something else: a faint sound like wind through reeds, as though air was moving through his body in ways that defied anatomy.

The other sisters avoided looking too closely at him. His skin was pale as parchment, veined with blue that seemed to pulse with its own light. Where his shoulder blades met, the feathers grew not from follicles but from fissures—fine seams in his back that had opened during birth and never healed. The skin around these openings was tender, raw, weeping a clear fluid that smelled of rain and crushed flowers.

The feathers themselves were unlike anything found in nature. They were translucent, almost glass-like, and when light passed through them they cast tiny rainbows on the stone walls. Sister Bernadine[3], who had studied natural philosophy before taking her vows, noted that they seemed to be growing not from his skin but through it, as though they originated somewhere deeper inside his body and were merely emerging at his back.

---

2   *"Erevale dear, are you writing?" "No, Mother Superior. Studying for vespers."*

3   *"Sister Bernadine likes to talk of philosophy. Father Bell calls it heresy. I wonder if God hates free thinkings."*

He was fed by hand. Goat's milk, soaked in muslin and pressed gently between his sealed lips. The first time Sister Agatha attempted this, she expected resistance. How could he swallow with his mouth fused shut? But the milk disappeared somehow, absorbed through his lips like water into dry earth. He suckled without sound, his throat working silently to draw in sustenance.

When he slept, his eyes moved behind their lids, rapid fluttering movements that suggested dreams more vivid than those of ordinary children. The sisters swore they heard hymns in languages they could not name—not aloud, but somehow transmitted through the air itself, humming in their bones like the residual vibration of struck tuning forks.

Sister Marie-Claire, who was sensitive to such things, claimed she could understand fragments of these dream-songs. They spoke of vast spaces, of flight, of a longing so profound it had weight and substance. They spoke of words that could only be told in silence, of voices that could only be heard by those who had forgotten how to listen.

They took this as a sign.

Not of holiness, exactly, but of something adjacent to it. Something that existed in the spaces between sacred and profane, between miracle and monstrosity.

Perhaps that was the beginning of his Hell.

Mother Superior consulted the archives, searching for precedent, for some record of similar births. She found references to changelings, to children born of angels and mortal women, to infants who served as vessels for divine communication. None matched exactly, but all shared common elements: silence, strange behaviour in animals and objects, the sense that reality bent slightly around them.

So, they moved Asael was moved from the reliquary wing

into the scriptorium, a long, narrow room with tall windows that let in the northern light preferred by scribes and illuminators. A feather had birthed him, after all—or rather, feathers had birthed him, feathers grew from him, feathers seemed to be as much a part of his essence as blood or bone. It was only right he reside in the highest point of the chapel. "Closer to the sky, perhaps he will fly away."

Wooden desks lined the walls, each equipped with inkwells, quills, and scrolls in various stages of completion. The air smelled of oak gall ink and sheep skin and the wax used to seal finished manuscripts. It was here that the sisters copied texts, illustrated prayer books, and maintained the correspondence that connected their small chapel to the larger world of faith and scholarship.

Through the years, his limbs lengthened in proportion, maintaining their bird-like delicacy. His hair, which had been nearly white at birth, darkened to the colour of storm clouds. The sealed mouth remained so, but the shape of it changed, becoming more defined, more expressive. Though he could not speak, his face was eloquent—joy and sorrow and curiosity flickering across his features like weather.

And still, he did not cry.

Sister Elene, despite her scientific training and natural scepticism, found herself drawn to his education. Perhaps it was curiosity about how a mind developed without speech. Perhaps it was motherly instinct—she had given up the possibility of children when she took her vows, and this strange, silent boy awakened something in her that had long been dormant.

She showed him how to hold books without damaging them[4], how to turn pages carefully with clean hands. She traced the shape of letters with her finger while he watched, demonstrating how meaning could be extracted from marks on parchment. She taught him to smell a page and know if it had been touched by heat or blood or prayer—each left its own signature scent that a trained nose could detect.

When Sister Elene placed his palm against a page of illuminated psalms, his fingers would trace the decorated capitals as though he could feel the gold leaf through his skin. His breathing would change, becoming deeper, more rhythmic, matching some internal tempo that seemed connected to the text itself.

It was through this that he learned to speak through gesture. He folded corners of cloth to communicate hunger—sharp, precise creases that somehow conveyed not just the desire for food but specific types: milk folded one way, bread another, honey in a pattern that resembled a flower. He pressed his forehead to glass when he wanted to be let outside, leaving faint impressions that looked like wing-shapes when the light hit them right.

When he desired something he could not name—comfort, perhaps, or understanding—he would curl up in his cot and pull the feathers from his back until his skin split again and new ones grew in their place.

---

4   *"Sister Aberdine once gifted me a book about swans. I wonder where I set it?"*

The moulting was painful, judging by his expressions, but he seemed driven to it by some compulsion stronger than discomfort. The discarded feathers were perfect, pristine, untouched by blood despite being torn from raw skin. Sister Agatha collected them, uncertain why but unable to simply dispose of something that felt so significant.

He left notes in the form of moulted down arranged like runes. Complex patterns spread across the floor of his cell each morning—spirals and geometric shapes and symbols that seemed to shift when viewed from different angles. They reminded Sister Agatha of the diagrams she had seen in books about natural philosophy, the charts used to map the movement of celestial bodies or the flow of humours through the human form.

The sisters swept them away each day, but they kept returning. More elaborate each time, more precise. As though the boy was learning to refine his language, to make his meaning clearer through repetition and variation.

Only Sister Elene kept a record. Despite, her age and the arthritis that made writing painful, she gathered each fallen feather and pressed it into the blank pages of an unused ledger. Underneath each, she scrawled what she believed he meant. Hunger. Ache. Rain. Touch. Otherness.

Her handwriting grew shakier as the months passed, but her dedication never wavered. She seemed to understand, in a way the others did not, that these feathers were a form of scripture. That the boy was writing himself into existence one moulted plume at a time, creating a gospel that could only be read by those willing to see language in forms other than words.

When she died—quietly, of old age, slumping over her writing desk during evening prayers—no one took her place. The ledger was filed away with her other belongings, and the systematic collection of feathers ceased.

III

The first sound he ever made was a sob, and it came on the day of Sister Elene's feast. It was not a formal celebration, for she had never been canonized, but a small remembrance organized by the sisters who had loved her. It was the first anniversary of her passing, and they wanted to honour the woman who had brought so many of them into the world, who had understood the boy in ways that others still struggled to comprehend.

A small procession had formed to mark the occasion. The sisters lit incense made from herbs she had grown in the chapel garden—lavender and rosemary and something else she had never named, something that bloomed only in shadow and smelled of honey and old books. They washed her empty cot with water blessed during the previous Easter and adorned it with flowers that had been her favourites: white roses and baby's breath and tiny blue forget-me-nots.

Someone placed a white feather at the centre of the arrangement, though no one knew where it came from. It was larger than any of the boy's moulted plumes, broader and more robust, with an iridescent quality that made it seem to glow in the candlelight. Sister Marie-Claire suggested it might have been one of Sister Elene's—saved from some previous encounter with the boy, preserved as a memento of her unique connection to him.

The boy watched from the doorway of the scriptorium. He had never shown interest in the sisters' activities before, content to remain in his corner with his books and his feathers and his silent contemplations. But today he stood at the threshold, his pale eyes fixed on the proceedings with an intensity that made several of the sisters uncomfortable.

He watched as they praised Sister Elene's memory. As they sang soft songs she had taught them—lullabies for difficult births, hymns for the dying, wordless melodies that seemed to ease pain in ways that medicine could not. As they poured wine onto the stone floor where she had once taught him to press his palms in ink, creating handprints that had faded but were still faintly visible if one knew where to look.

And then he wept.

It was not a loud sob. It came from his throat like oil, thick and resistant, forced through passages that were not designed for sound. His mouth remained sealed, but the sound pushed through his nose, his ribs, the gap between his spine where his wings attached to muscle and bone. A guttural mourning that didn't sound like a child at all, but like something older. Something that had been grieving for centuries and had finally found voice.

The sisters fell silent.[5] One of them dropped the incense boat, sending a cloud of aromatic smoke spiralling toward the vaulted ceiling. Another crossed herself twice, then a third time, as though the first two attempts had not been sufficient protection against whatever she was witnessing.

The sound continued for several minutes—not growing louder, but deepening, developing harmonics that seemed to resonate in the stone walls themselves. It was not entirely human, but it was entirely grief. Pure, distilled sorrow given form and substance.

He fell to his knees as the sound finally faded, and from his back—six feathers fell. Not moulted in the usual way, but released

---

5   *"Is it normal to feel guilty when you cry? Like you don't have the right? Like your tears take away from someone else's hurt?"*

36

all at once, dropping like snow onto the stone floor.

From that day forward, the sisters avoided him entirely.

The transformation was immediate and absolute. Where once they had been curious about his nature, now they were disturbed. Where once they had been protective, now they were wary. The sob had been too raw, too powerful, too much like the voice of something that should not have voice.

They moved him from the scriptorium into the east transept, into a cell without windows. It was smaller than his previous quarters, darker, lined with stone that wept moisture in the winter months. His meals were left on a tray outside the door. His bedding was changed only when he left it piled in the corridor, folded in the precise patterns he used to communicate his needs. Even his name, once a divine gift, was exchanged for simply 'the boy'.

He had become, they whispered when they thought he could not hear, too near to divine. Which is to say; too near to monstrous. For divinity and monstrosity, they were beginning to understand, were often the same phenomenon viewed from different perspectives.

No one knew what to make of the sob. It felt like it had echoed for hours after he made it, bouncing off the stone walls and returning in waves of diminishing intensity. The chapel rang with it. The bell rope untethered itself that night and was found coiled at the chapel door like a snake, its bronze bell lying silent on the ground despite showing no signs of having been cut or damaged.

Other strange things happened in the days that followed. The wine they had poured for Sister Elene's memorial began to bubble and ferment, turning the stone floor purple-black with stains that resembled wing-shapes. The flowers on her cot bloomed out of season, growing larger and more vibrant than nature should have allowed. The white feather disappeared entirely, though careful searches revealed no trace of where it might have gone.

He did not sob again.

But he began to write.

Not in gesture. Not in feather arrangements. Not in the wordless communication he had developed over his years in the chapel.

In ink.

The first manuscript page was found folded beneath his dinner tray three days after his relocation to the east transept. It bore no title, no signature, no indication of how he had managed to write it—who had given him pen and ink? Yet there it was. A single sheet covered in the clumsy script of a child.

It contained only a single passage;

"Once, there was a boy with wings in his throat. He could not speak, for his voice was lined with barbs and bone. But those who listened long enough swore they remembered nothing else afterward. Not their name. Not their grief. Only the sound of silence, and the fluttering of something vast and frightened behind it."

Sister Agatha discovered the page when she came to collect his empty tray. She read it three times before the words fully registered, then carried it to Mother Superior with hands that trembled slightly. Neither of them could explain how he had written it. Neither of them could deny that the handwriting was his—they had seen him practice letters, had watched him trace characters in dust and crumbs and the condensation on his washbasin.

But this was different. This was story. This was voice made manifest on parchment, silence transformed into words that seemed to pulse with their own life.

More pages appeared over the following days. They would

find them in unexpected places—folded into their prayer books, slipped under their cell doors, pressed between the pages of manuscripts they were copying. Each contained fragments of the same story: the boy with wings in his throat, the people who listened and forgot, the terrible price of being heard.

The writing grew more elaborate with each iteration. Detailed descriptions of the boy's isolation, his attempts to communicate, the gradual erasure of those who tried to understand him. It was beautiful writing—lyrical, haunting, touched with an otherworldly quality that made it impossible to dismiss as mere fiction.

So they were beginning to suspect it was not fiction at all, but rather, prophecy.

And in the east transept, behind a door that was never locked but somehow never opened easily, the boy continued to write. His sealed mouth worked silently as he shaped words on pages that materialized from nothing, telling the story of his own becoming, documenting his transformation from child to legend to something that existed in the spaces between words.

He was no longer just the boy who could not speak.

He was becoming The Boy whose silence spoke louder than any voice.

And in the growing collection of pages, a larger story was beginning to emerge. A story about the cost of being seen, the danger of being understood, the terrible weight of carrying voices that were never meant to be heard.

It would be years before anyone understood what he was trying to tell them.

By then, it would be too late to listen.

In the weeks that followed, when his own silence grew too heavy to bear, he tried shaping sounds again. Not sobs nor hymns, only fragments—syllables he had seen written in the books Sister Elene had traced with him.

And thus, it began as a fissure.

A hairline seam running along the line of his lips, tender and inflamed. At first the sisters thought it was chapping, the consequence of dry winter air and his refusal to eat more than what was necessary. But the seam did not heal. Each morning it deepened, the skin parting in the smallest of increments, as though his body had decided to unpick itself stitch by stitch.

The crack widened.

When he pressed his tongue against it, it bled. Thin threads of scarlet welled up and traced the curve of his chin. His tongue itself was wrong—longer than it should have been, narrow, pale, and feathered. Not like hair, not like fur, but like the vanes of a bird's wing shaved down to their smallest size. When he rasped against the inside of his lips, the sisters swore they could hear it; a dry, papery hiss, like quills dragged across stone.

When the seam had torn enough for the pointed tip of his tongue to poke through, he began to spit up down. Tiny clumps of white, wet and matted, tangled with streaks of blood. They collected on his bedding, in the corners of his cell, in the bowls of milk left for him. Sister Agatha noted them clinically at first, storing them in small jars, but after the third week she swept them away in silence, unable to bear the implications.

At night, his body convulsed. He writhed on his cot, jaw straining against skin that wanted to stay closed. The seam split further at the corners, crooked lines tugging his face into the semblance of a grin. Each new tear made a sound like cloth ripping, soft but unmistakable in the quiet of the transept.

The sisters began avoiding the night watch. They feared the noises. The wet rasp of his tongue thrashing against its cage, the drip of blood onto stone, the muffled gasps that were not sobs but something more desperate.

By the second month, his lips had pulled apart far enough that the glint of teeth was visible. Too white, too perfect, too new— as though they had been waiting all along behind the sealed flesh. They gleamed even in candlelight, the enamel catching flame as if polished.

By the third month, his jaw had begun to loosen. He could stretch his mouth wider than any child should, the hinge clicking softly when he yawned, when he twisted in his sleep, when he mouthed silent words against the wall of his cell. The tongue feathered more each day. Sometimes he gagged on it, hacking feathers from his throat, his small body shaking until pale plumes spewed from between his lips and floated across the room covered in spittle.

The sisters began to whisper that he was unravelling. That his silence had not been mercy, but dam. That when it broke, it would drown them.

And then spring came.

And by then, his mouth was open.

It, like the rest of him, was unnatural. His jaw stretched too far, his teeth too even, his tongue restless and bristling. His lips were always bloodied at the edges, as though even in stillness they were tearing wider.

This was the mouth with which he would speak., but the sisters did not yet realize what his voice could do. They believed the sob was mourning, grief pressed through a body not meant for sound. They did not yet know it was dangerous.

The Boy learned before they did. And the first time he spoke to another, it was to a child.

A pilgrim's son, small enough to wander the cloisters unnoticed, had slipped into the east transept one morning when the sisters were occupied with lauds. He carried a crust of bread, half-eaten, and stared at The Boy as if looking at a painting come alive. His eyes were bright, curious, not yet lined with devotional fear the way his elders' were.

The Boy wanted desperately to answer that gaze.

So he forced a word. Just one. The name the child had given when asked by a sister the day before.

"Peter."

And then Peter stilled.

Recognition drained from his face. His eyes—once bright—seemed to empty, as though someone had poured them out. He blinked once. Twice. And then his voice came, thin, frightened, unravelling as fast as the bread crust falling from his hand.

"Pe…ter?" he asked.

His voice trembled.

"I am… Where… I…?"

He looked around the transept as though it had become alien stone. His small body shook. His sobs rose sharp and ragged. He clutched at his head, beating his temples with his fists as if to strike memory back into place.

By the time the sisters rushed in, their psalm still clinging to the air, the child was inconsolable. He clung to their skirts, crying out for a woman no one had ever known, a name none of them recognized, a home that no longer existed even in his own mind.

The Boy sat frozen, trembling with the word still burning in his throat. He tried to swallow it back, to force it down into marrow where it belonged, where it could not cut anyone else. But the harm was done. He had spoken. And he had learned the consequences.

The sisters whispered that the child was seized by vision, that angels had passed him. They spoked in hushes, not daring to accuse The Boy. Not yet.

But he knew.

So he said nothing more.

Not in the secrecy of his cell, not in the emptiness of midnight, not even when the air itself seemed to beg for release. He sealed his lips with silence, pressing every syllable back into the bone of his body.

And he carried the knowledge of what his voice could do.

That with one word, he could unmake the living.

And yet, the urge to speak remained. It pulsed in his lips, beat against his teeth, throbbed in his throat like wings against a locked door. He turned it elsewhere.

He wrote.

Each page carried what he could no longer risk saying. Each word a carving of silence, each line a way of bleeding without harm. The sisters found the pages scattered everywhere—beneath trays, slipped into prayer books, pressed into stone cracks.

When Sister Agatha brought them to Father Lucien, he read them in silence. By the third page, his hands trembled. "These are not stories," he whispered. "These are visions."

From then on, every scrap of writing was taken. Gathered with reverence, carried away as though it were already relic. He was moved from his small cell to a chamber with a desk, parchment, quills cut from swan feathers. The sisters bowed as they entered, calling him "blessed," though they still feared his eyes.

The Boy wrote because it was safer than speaking, and because the pages filled the hollow of his chest. But he noticed how quickly they vanished into other hands. How they were copied, glossed, made heavier with meaning not his own.

He did not see visions. He only saw loneliness pressed into paper, silence poured into shape. To him, the words were bleeding. To them, they were scripture.

And he thought: perhaps sainthood begins not with miracles, but with the careful theft of what makes a boy human.[6]

---

6   *"Am I still human?"*

IV

The garden was the only place the sisters left unattended.

They weeded it at dawn, gathering herbs and root vegetables before the day's bells began their ancient chorus, but by afternoon the cloister paths were empty, save for the slow drip of rainwater from stone gutters worn smooth by centuries of weather and the crows that settled on the wall to pick at fallen seed. The birds watched with eyes like black glass, silent witnesses to the chapel's secrets. The Boy found himself there often, drawn by something he could not name—a hunger for spaces unblessed, untouched by the weight of reverent stares. Not in open view—he never risked being seen, never allowed his presence to stain their careful rituals—but in the hollow of the ancient yew hedge, pressed between branches that scratched his pale arms and left their bitter, resinous scent embedded in his skin like a penance.

The hedge was older than the chapel itself, its roots drinking from soil that had known other gods, other silences. Here, tucked between its twisted limbs, he could breathe without ceremony. The feathers in his throat settled into quieter rhythms, no longer straining against the constant pressure of observation. He could exist, for precious moments, as something other than… whatever he was.

It was there he saw her first.

A girl.

She moved with none of the measured stiffness of the sisters, none of the calculated reverence of priests who had forgotten the difference between devotion and performance. Her hair was loose, dark curls sticking to her cheeks where honest sweat had dampened them, and she knelt barefoot in the black soil as though it belonged to her—or she to it. Her hands worked the earth with familiarity, fingers dark with loam, nails crescented with the honest dirt of labour. He thought, for a moment, she was younger than him. Then older. Her body seemed caught between the ages, one moment childlike in its easy grace, the next blooming toward womanhood with the urgent tenderness of spring shoots, as if she were stitched from different seasons, different hungers.

She sang while she worked. Not hymns—never the careful, hollow hymns that echoed through the chapel's vaulted spaces—but crooked little melodies, folk songs with words that did not carry sense so much as rhythm, so much as joy. The sound reached him through the hedge, thin but startling as birdsong, and he felt the feathers in his throat stir restlessly, answering like a flock disturbed by distant thunder. They pressed against his palate, eager and warm, as though they remembered flight.

The Boy froze, one hand pressed to his throat where the movement fluttered beneath his skin. He was used to being hidden, to being feared, to silence pressing in on all sides like a coffin lined with velvet. He was not used to being tempted by voice, by the dangerous sweetness of another's song calling to the wings that lived beneath his tongue.

The girl paused her melody long enough to glance toward the hedge, her head tilted like a sparrow listening for rain. "I see you."

His body stiffened, every muscle drawing tight as bowstring. The feathers in his throat went still, sensing danger in the way prey senses the shadow of hawks.

She smiled. Not cruelly, not with the terrible gentleness of those who called him blessed, but with the simple delight of discovery—the way children smiled at butterflies or first snow. "Don't be afraid. I won't tell them."

He did not move. Could not move. Fear and longing warred in his chest, each breath a small betrayal of the silence he had been taught to carry like sacrament.

She returned to her weeding, humming once more, her voice threading through the afternoon air like golden thread through dark cloth. After a while, she began to speak—not to him directly, but aloud, as though the garden itself were her audience, as though the carrots and beans might carry her words to whatever gods still listened in this forgotten corner of the world. She told half-stories about her family; a brother who had run away to sea with nothing but his father's coat and a pocketful of stolen bread, a mother who baked loaves that tasted of woodsmoke and summer mornings, a father who gambled away their mule and came home drunk, singing ballads that made her mother weep. The sisters had taken her in two winters ago, she said, when the cold had claimed her mother and her father had disappeared into his bottles like a man drowning in reverse.

She was not a novice, not yet old enough for such binding vows, but she lingered among the sisters like a stray bird seeking rafters to roost in, earning her keep with kitchen work and garden tending, with the small labours that kept holy places human.

The Boy listened with the desperate attention of the starved, each word falling into him like drops of water on parched earth, soaking into places that had been dry so long he had forgotten they could drink. Her voice carried the taste of the world beyond these walls—salt air and market days, laughter that rang without echo, tears shed for reasons other than divine rapture.

Every afternoon thereafter, he returned to the. And every afternoon, she spoke to him, though she never turned her head or raised her voice above the level of confession. It was their secret ritual, as sacred as any the chapel housed.

She would speak, he would listen. The world would turn, and for an hour each day, he would remember what it felt like to be human.

Weeks passed this way, each afternoon a small rebellion against the weight of his sanctification.[7]

Sometimes, she brought him small gifts, slipping them between the branches when no sister's eye might catch the movement. A crust of bread still warm from the ovens, a sprig of mint that made his throat flutter with something like joy, a scrap of blue ribbon she had found near the laundry lines, bright as summer sky against the chapel's grey stones. He accepted them wordlessly, tucking them into his sleeves like contraband, like prayers offered to gods whose names he did not know. In return, he left feathers—not his moulted down, which would have been too intimate, too much like bleeding—but the smallest plumes he could spare without opening wounds. Tiny things, soft as whispers, that grew from the edges of his collarbone where the sisters rarely looked.

She collected them eagerly, weaving them into her dark hair or stitching them into the hem of her rough tunic with careful, secret stitches. They caught the light when she moved, winking like captured starlight, like hope made manifest in thread and bone.

She called him her shadow, her garden ghost, her secret saint.

He never wrote her name in his pages, even when his fingers ached to shape the letters. He never offered her up to the chapel's hunger, never let the sisters' eyes fall upon her like sunlight through a lens, burning whatever it touched into ash and memory. She was his alone, a secret friendship tucked away like contraband beneath

---

7   *"I didn't mean to write it like that. It only came out that way because I was tired."*

48

the floorboards of his silence, like love hidden in the spaces between ribs.

But one afternoon, after a particularly harsh rain, she found him bolder than usual. Instead of hiding in the hedge like some woodland creature afraid of human touch, he stepped out into the grey light, his bare feet silent on the wet earth. His mouth was half-healed that day, the edges scabbed over but still too raw to close comfortably. He kept his lips parted just enough to breathe without pain, just enough to taste the rain-sweet air.

But she did not flinch at the sight of him. Not at his pallor, not at the strange angles of his bones, not at the way small feathers sometimes drifted from his robes like tears made solid.

"You're beautiful." She said simply, her voice carrying the weight of truth spoken without thought, without calculation.

The words struck him hard, like lightning finding its way to earth through the tallest tree. No one had ever named him that way—not relic, not blessed, not vessel, not the hollow thing they poured their devotions into—but... beautiful. Human and more than human, flesh and spirit speaking to flesh and spirit, spoken without fear, without the terrible reverence that turned love into worship and worship into cage.

He wanted to thank her.

The urge burned in him like fever, like the first touch of spring after winter's long death. He felt it in his marrow, in the seams of his back where new feathers pushed through skin like prayers made manifest, in the ache of his jaw where his mouth had split itself open to house the unspeakable.

His body trembled with the need to answer, to offer her something other than silence, something more than the mute devotion of an icon carved from flesh and longing. To be, for one moment, more than sacred. To be grateful. To be damned, if damnation was the price of speech.

So he forgot himself. Forgot the warnings whispered in corridors, forgot the weight of wings beating beneath his tongue, forgot everything but the girl before him and the words burning in his chest.

He leaned closer, close enough to see the flecks of gold in her brown eyes, close enough to smell the earth on her skin. His lips bled when they shaped themselves around the syllables, splitting like overripe fruit, like wounds that had never properly healed.

"Thank you."

It was no louder than a sigh, no stronger than the whisper of wind through wheat, but the sound was terrible beyond imagining.

Air tore through his throat like a blade through silk, rattling the feathered tongue until it hissed and whistled like a hundred wings beating at once in the confines of a too-small cage. The syllables warped as they escaped, carrying with them not gratitude but erasure, not blessing but curse. The words transformed in the space between his mouth and her ears, becoming something hungry, something that devoured rather than offered, something that took away instead of giving thanks.

The girl blinked.

Once.

Twice. Slow and confused, like someone waking from dreams.

Her smile faltered, cracking like ice in spring. Confusion clouded her features, as if someone had snatched her reflection from the surface of a still pond, leaving only ripples and distortion. She looked down at her hands, at the small feathers she clutched, and her breath quickened with the first touch of panic.

"Where—" she began, then stopped, the word dying half-formed on her tongue.

Her gaze swept the garden, wide and panicked, searching for something she could not name but knew was missing. She pressed her fists against her temples, fingers digging into skin as though trying to anchor herself in the pain, as though pain might call back what speech had stolen. "Who—what am I doing here? Where's... who—" Her voice broke into ragged gasps, the sound of something precious shattering against stone.

She dropped the feathers, and they fell like the remnants of dreams upon waking.

The Boy reached for her with trembling hands, but she recoiled as though touched by flame, stumbling backward into the damp earth, her eyes wide with the terror of facing the monstrous stranger she had known moments before. The recognition was gone from her face, wiped clean as a slate, leaving only fear and confusion and disgust where tenderness had once lived.

He said nothing more. Could say nothing more. The wings in his throat had settled back into stillness, sated by their feeding, by the memory they had consumed like bread broken and shared.

The sisters found her wandering near the, weeping and incoherent, her hair full of feathers she could not remember gathering. They led her back inside with gentle hands and worried murmurs, speaking of fevers and bad air, of the fragility of children who had lost too much too young to bear the weight of more loss. They pressed rosaries into her palms and laid her on cool linens, whispering prayers that did not answer the real absence, that could not call back what had been devoured.

The Boy returned to his hedge alone, his mouth still bleeding, still tasting of words that should never have been spoken.

Her ribbon still lay in the grass where she had dropped it,

a scrap of blue bright as summer sky against the dark earth. He picked it up shakily, wound it carefully around his finger until it bit into the skin, and tucked it into the lining of his robe where it would rest against his heart like a thorn, a reminder of the last piece of something beautiful he had destroyed with love.

The feathers she had carried remained scattered across the soil, already sodden from the rain. By morning, they would be pulp, indistinguishable from the loam that fed the garden's roots.

That night he wrote a page, his hand moving across the parchment like something possessed.

It appeared beneath the sisters' prayer books at lauds, pressed like a curse between worn leaves that had absorbed decades of whispered devotions. The script was sharper than before, the ink darker, each letter carved with the precision of pain given form. The words seemed to bleed across the page, edged with loss.

"Once, there was a boy who spoke thank you, and it devoured the one he loved. Her name was written in feathers, but feathers are made to be lost. Now the wind carries her, and no one remembers her face but him. This is the price of holy speech; to speak is to steal. To love is to unmake. To be grateful is to become the very silence you break."

The sisters did not understand, could not understand. They whispered of allegory, of divine parable, of warnings meant for future generations who might walk similar paths. They pressed it between glass and gold, another relic for their collection, another piece of the holy boy's divine madness.

They called it vision.

They called it prophecy.

He called it grief.

It was loss, crystallized into words that cut like glass, like memory made sharp enough to draw blood. His first attempt at love, devoured by the very mouth meant to return it, consumed by the blessing that was also curse, the gift that was also burden.

He never returned to the garden. Never allowed the sun to warm his face in those unguarded spaces. Never let himself forget that even in Eden, serpents spoke with honeyed tongues.

He never allowed himself to be beautiful again.

V

Dreams were merciless, but they did not carry remnants of the girl. They gave him only wings, throats, mouths unseaming themselves in endless corridors of teeth. He woke each morning gasping, lips torn wider, blood dried in the corners like wax from a spent candle. Her name lived nowhere but in his marrow, her memory forever lodged in his throat.

But silence was not peace. It pressed on him heavier than chains. A silence that was imposed onto him and fused into his flesh like iron into bone.

He had learned what his words could do. He had seen it in Peter.

Had seen it when her face collapse into bewilderment.

Had watched memory flake away like paint.

And yet—the urge remained. His throat itched with it, seethed with it, a hunger more relentless than fasting, more cruel than pain.

The sensation had grown worse with each passing day. Beneath the skin of his neck, he could feel them writhing—feathers pressing outward like tiny blades, seeking air, seeking voice. They scraped against the inside of his throat when he swallowed, rustled wetly when he breathed. Sometimes he could taste their metallic tang on his tongue, the flavour of copper and down mingling with his own saliva until he could not tell where his body ended and the curse began.

One night, unable to bear the weight of his own quiet, he rose from his cot. His cell was black save for the dim oil lamp left by the sisters, its flame stuttering in the damp air. The wick had burned low, casting trembling shadows that danced across the stone walls like living things. On the far wall, a mirror hung crooked, one of the few objects left to him when they moved him from the scriptorium. The sisters claimed it was there for penance—that to see one's own reflection was to confront sin.

He approached it slowly, bare feet silent on the cold stone.

The glass did not greet him kindly. His face was gaunt, shadowed, lips fissured where they had torn themselves open to form that cursed thank you. The corners of his mouth were scabbed black, the skin bruised purple and yellow from weeks of strain. His jaw looked somehow too wide yet too narrow, and when he breathed, feathers shivered against his teeth, pale and translucent, slick with blood and bile. Dark veins had begun to spider outward from the corners of his mouth, threading under his skin like ink spilled through water.

He hated it.

He hated the reflection[8], the reminder that his silence was not holy but monstrous, that his mouth was no longer a child's but a wound that never healed. The thing staring back at him was no longer the boy who had been birthed in these halls and named after an angel. This was something else.

Something growing

Something becoming.

He wanted to claw it shut again. To be rid of it entirely.

So he opened his mouth, and his fingers reached into his

---

8   *"I wonder how I look in the eyes of others. I wonder if my reflection tells lies and my skin is peeling."*

throat.

The fissures where his tongue rooted itself were tender, pulsing faintly like living seams. He could feel the heartbeat of the feathers beneath his skin, each one a separate entity seeking escape. His nails dug into the soft flesh, feeling them sink deep into the yielding tissue.

The skin parted like overripe fruit, the feathers quivering against his fingers as he gripped them shakily and pulled. His body convulsed as the clot of wet feathers tore loose, long as his palm and still slick at the root where flesh had grown to anchor it.

The pain was immediate, a searing so hot it blinded him for a moment and threatened his consciousness.

Sinew and membrane stretched like spider silk before snapping, releasing a spray of crimson that painted the mirror's surface. He gagged, choking on blood and plume as more followed—barbed, tangled, dragging chunks of raw flesh with them as they came. Each feather was rooted deep, threaded through muscle and cartilage, and as he pulled them free, he could feel his throat reshaping itself, the cavity growing wider, deeper.

Blood poured from his mouth in streams, pooling at his feet and spreading across the stone floor in dark, sticky puddles. The metallic scent filled the air, thick and cloying, mingling with the stench of torn tissue. Still he pulled, desperate to unmake himself, to carve the silence out by its roots. When the inside had cleared, when the feathers no longer choked him from the inside, he turned his attention to the outer ones.

His fingers tremored and slippery with gore, grabbed defiantly at the feathers around his throat and tore at them in clumps. His senses were clouded, tears mingling with the scent of his own raw flesh and pain stroking every nerve made each grip more precarious, but he did not stop.

Feathers filled the cell, clinging to his arms, matting in his hair, sticking wetly to the walls where they splattered, as if ripping them out made them desperate to imprison him in them some other way. Some were pristine white, others stained russet and black with blood. The larger ones bore strips of pink flesh at their roots, glistening membranes that had once connected them to his throat. Blood pooled in the cracks of the stone floor, dark and glistening, smelling of iron and rot and something else—something sweet and corrupt, like flowers left too long in water.

When at last his throat was raw and gaping, he staggered forward. The wound gaped like a second mouth, edges ragged and weeping. He could see into the cavity now, see the pale curve of his spine gleaming wetly in the lamplight, see the torn muscles contracting with each heartbeat. And his reflection stared back at him—not boy, not angel, but something unravelling. The feathers within him had not stopped. They writhed still, pressing against the torn cavity, eager to spill forth again. New growths were already emerging, tiny white points pushing through the bloody tissue like teeth through gums.

His mouth opened.

The mirror fogged instantly, as though his breath carried winter. But this was no ordinary exhalation. It came thick with blood spray, droplets of crimson misting the glass and running down in long streaks. His exhale spread across the surface like frost crawling outward from a shattered vein, leaving spiderweb cracks in its wake.

And then he spoke.

Not words exactly—shapes, syllables bent wrong by the blood in his mouth and the fluttering of feathered tongue. The sound was a rasp, a scream caught inside a hymn, a noise that had never been meant for human air. Blood bubbled from the gaping wound in his throat with each syllable, frothing pink where it mixed with saliva and bile. The sound itself seemed to have weight, seemed to press against the walls of the cell with physical force.

The mirror buckled.

Its surface rippled as though struck by stone. His reflection smeared and warped, eyes sliding out of place, mouth stretching far beyond the edges of his jaw. The feathers he had torn scattered against the glass and seemed to pass through it, embedding themselves on the other side, where they fluttered as though suspended in water. But now they were not clean white—they dripped with flesh, trailing streamers of blood that painted the mirror's reverse surface in abstract patterns of crimson and black.

He watched, horrified, as the reflection twisted.

The boy in the mirror no longer mirrored him. Its mouth gaped wider, revealing not teeth but rows of feathered points that gleamed like wet bone. Its tongue unfurled into endless pale ribbons, each one tipped with barbs that caught the light. Blood ran from its eyes like tears, and its throat had become a cavern, lined with pulsing flesh and sprouting wings. Feathers sprouted from its cheeks, its forehead, its eyes, until the face dissolved entirely into wings pressing outward, wings made of flesh and quills and blood, wings that beat against the glass with wet, meaty sounds.

The sound he made reverberated back at him, doubled and inverted, a grotesque harmony that set the glass trembling in its frame. Each note was accompanied by a fresh gush of blood from his throat, the liquid spraying across the cell in arterial arcs. He could not tell if he was still speaking or if the mirror had learned to speak for him. His own voice folded over itself until the cell rang with something that was not sound but force, a pressure that pushed against his chest, his lungs, his skull.

Cracks bloomed across the glass.

They spidered outward from the reflection's mouth, thin at first, then widening. Each new fracture carried with it a spray of blood that was not his—darker, thicker, reeking of decay. The blood ran down the mirror's surface in rivulets that left stains like rust, pooling at the base of the frame where it began to coagulate into dark, jelly-like clots. His reflection continued to convulse, feathers bursting from it in violent plumes, each eruption accompanied by gouts of viscera that splattered against the inside of the glass. It no longer resembled a boy at all but some grotesque icon, a martyr's painting smeared by centuries of neglect and corruption.

The boy staggered back. His throat was raw, bloodied, clogged with the feathers that had not yet been expelled. Fresh growth pushed through the wounds like maggots through carrion, pale and writhing. He tried to breathe, but every inhale rattled with papery rustling and the wet gurgle of blood filling his lungs. Every exhale whistled like a bird's dying call, spraying fine droplets of gore into the air. His knees buckled, and he fell into the nest of bloody plumes he had made on the floor, the feathers squelching beneath his weight and releasing fresh waves of metallic stench.

Still the mirror warped.

The cracks widened until shards fell, shattering on stone with sounds like breaking bones. Each shard that hit the ground showed a different reflection; his face sobbing, blood screaming through a throat lined with feathers, silent and drowning in his own butchery, winged and crucified on an altar of bone. His throat in violent bloom, ribs splitting to reveal nests of beating wings, mouth gaping wide enough to swallow light itself. He wanted to cover his eyes, but even the shards cut through his closed lids, the images burning themselves into his vision. The mirror showed him as he was and as he would become, fractured into endless futures that all ended in silence—the silence of the grave, the silence of the altar, the silence of the relic he was destined to become.

And then—nothing.

The mirror collapsed inward, as though drawn into itself.

The last of the glass fell, leaving only an empty frame that seemed to yawn like a mouth, like a wound, like a doorway to nowhere. The sudden quiet felt oppressive after the cacophony, broken only by the steady drip of blood from the ceiling where it had splattered, and the wet sound of his own laboured breathing.

The Boy lay gasping among the feathers, blood pooling beneath him in an ever-widening lake. His throat throbbed, not with relief but with new hunger, new pressure, the promise that more would grow, more would tear, more would demand to be spoken. The wounds in his neck pulsed with their own rhythm, opening and closing like gills, like mouths seeking air. He pressed his hands to his neck, desperate to hold himself shut, but the seams pulsed against his palms like a second heartbeat, and fresh blood seeped between his fingers in warm, sticky streams.

He knew now, he could never unmake himself.

He could only break further.

And the world with him.

VI

The cell breathed with him, damp stone swelling and shrinking as if the walls had become ribs, the mortar between them pulsing like sinew stretched taut. The feathers he had torn from his throat littered the floor like snow rotted to ash, their delicate barbs clotted together with blood that had darkened to the colour of communion wine. Each feather caught what little light filtered through the narrow window, casting fractured rainbows across the grey stone—beautiful and terrible, like relics of some failed angel.

He lay in the midst of them until his body grew cold, until the blood beneath him had begun to congeal and stick to his skin like a second flesh. The pain in his throat had dulled to a persistent ache, a hollow throb that matched the rhythm of his heartbeat. He could no longer tell if he had died and woken again, if this was purgatory or simply another dawn he had survived against all expectation and desire.

But when he lifted his head, when his lips parted and he heard nothing come—not breath, not whisper, not even the faintest rustle of remaining feathers—he knew he had not died. He had survived against his will, and somehow that felt heavier than death, more burdensome than the weight of wings that had once filled his throat like unspoken hymns.

He rose, his limbs stiff and trembling like those of an old man, though he hadn't even seen fifteen summers. The movement sent fresh pain shooting through his neck and jaw, and for a moment he swayed, pressing one bloodied hand against the wall for support. The stone was cold beneath his palm, solid and unforgiving, a reminder that this world was real and would not dissolve at his touch like the dreams that had sustained him.

There was no basin to wash in, only a clay jar half-filled with water left from the sisters' morning visit—water meant for drinking, not cleansing, but it would have to serve. He lifted the jar with both hands, his fingers leaving crimson prints on its rough surface, and tipped it over his head. The shock of its chill stung his wounds clean, each drop like a tiny blessing or curse as it traced the lines of dried blood down his throat. The water streamed down his chest in red rivulets, diluting the gore until it ran pink as watered wine, pooling among the broken feathers at his feet and turning them into a sodden mass of beauty and ruin.

He tore linen from his bedding to make bandages, the fabric splitting with a sound like prayer books being torn. The sheets had been white once, pristine as altar cloth, but now they would serve a different sacrament. He wound strips around his throat, covering the raw wounds where feathers had been rooted, then wrapped his jaw and the corners of his mouth where the largest plumes had pushed through. The cloth darkened quickly with fresh seepage but held, creating a cocoon of white around the devastation. When he caught his reflection in the water jar's curved surface, he looked like a saint prepared for martyrdom. Or perhaps a corpse dressed for burial.

From a chest in the corner—carved with images of doves and olive branches, a mockery now—he drew the fresh clothes they had given him weeks earlier. Plain tunic the colour of undyed wool, woollen trousers that scratched against his skin, and a cloak meant for winter errands he had never been allowed to run, its fabric heavy as penance. He pulled them on with clumsy fingers, each movement dragging like a ritual performed by one who had forgotten its meaning. The tunic hung loose on his frame, hiding the bandages but not their bulk. The cloak's hood fell forward when he lifted it, casting his face into shadow deep as a confessional.

For the feathers that still quivered at the seams of his lips—the stubborn few that had refused to be torn free, that pressed against his mouth like secrets demanding voice—he wound another cloth over his mouth and nose, pulling it tight until the urge to speak pressed against it like a caged bird beating its wings against wire. He bound himself into silence more complete than any vow, more final than any grave.

When he stepped from the cell, the transept stretched before him darker than he had ever known it. The oil lamps that usually burned through the night had guttered out, their wicks drowned in their own wax, leaving only the memory of light lingering in the air like incense. The stones beneath his feet were slick with the night's damp and something else—a trail of blood he had left in his earlier wanderings, drops that had fallen from his wounds like breadcrumbs marking a path he could no longer remember walking. No sister stood guard at her accustomed post, no bell tolled the hours. The very air seemed to hold its breath, as though the chapel itself conspired in his departure.

He walked in solitude through corridors that had never known such emptiness, his footsteps echoing off vaulted ceilings that seemed to stretch into infinity. The familiar statues of saints watched him pass with stone eyes that reflected no recognition, their carved faces serene in their ignorance. They had witnessed countless confessions, countless prayers, countless acts of devotion, but tonight they would see something new—a relic walking away from its own shrine.

The nave yawned open before him like the mouth of some great beast, its vaulted ceiling lost to shadow so complete it might have opened onto the star-scattered void itself. Candles flickered at the altar, their flames dancing as though stirred by breath that came from no living lung. They were the only light left to guide him, a constellation of fire that seemed to pulse in rhythm with the ache in his throat. The pews stretched in perfect rows on either side, their wood polished by centuries of hands to a gleam like dark water. Tonight they seemed to lean inward, as though the building itself wished to hear his departure, to witness this final sacrament.

The air carried the lingering sweetness of frankincense and myrrh, the ghostly presence of a thousand masses said and sung within these walls. Beneath that sacred perfume lay something else—the copper tang of his own blood, the mustiness of feathers, the salt of tears he had never been permitted to shed openly. It was the smell of martyrdom, of transformation, of something precious being destroyed in service of something greater.

He paused at the threshold of the altar rail, its brass worn smooth by countless hands that had gripped it in prayer or desperation. His breath came shallow and quick, fogging the cloth over his mouth with each exhalation. For a moment he considered turning back, returning to his cell, accepting whatever fate the sisters had planned for him. But the thought lasted only as long as a candle flame in wind.

He debated writing a letter, a note, some explanation that might survive when memory failed. His fingers twitched toward the small writing desk where he had once composed psalms under Sister Agatha's watchful eye. But he knew too well that there was no need. Words on paper would fade like everything else he touched. They wouldn't remember anyway—not his face, not his name, not the sound of wings beating in a human throat.

And so he prayed instead, mouthing the words through cloth and bandages, feeling them vibrate against the remaining feathers that lined his mouth like thorns.

He spoke, for the first time, with the conscious intention to devour memories. To erase himself from their minds as completely as he would erase himself from their sight. Each word was both blessing and curse, each syllable a small death.

Pater noster, qui es in caelis, sanctificetur nomen tuum.

The Latin rolled off his tongue like water over stones, familiar from years of listening to sermons and prayers and the clicking of rosary beads. The words were not his own—they belonged to centuries of faithful, to martyrs and saints and sinners alike—but tonight they steadied him, tasting of blood and feathers and something indefinably sacred.

The stones around him seemed to weep, moisture beading on their surface as though the chapel itself mourned. His whispers carried through the corridors like wind through a forest, bouncing off walls and pillars until they became echoes of echoes, a prayer folded back upon itself until it was both question and answer.

Adveniat regnum tuum. Fiat voluntas tua, sicut in caelo et in terra.

He walked the centre aisle slowly, each step measured as if to match the cadence of the prayer, as if his movement were itself a form of worship. The worn stones beneath his feet had been polished smooth by countless processions—brides and grooms, priests and penitents, the dying carried toward final rites. Tonight they supported his own procession of one, his journey from sanctuary to exile. The hood shadowed his face like a monk's cowl, the bandages muffled the rasp of his breath until it sounded like wind through autumn leaves. Behind him, feathers fell like snow. Like the scattered pages of a book being torn apart by invisible hands. No one would remember to follow the trail they left.

Panem nostrum quotidianum da nobis hodie.

The words felt heavier now, weighted with irony. Daily bread—but what nourishment had this place ever truly offered him? What sustenance beyond the bitter communion of worship and suffering? His stomach cramped with hunger he had learned to ignore, but tonight the emptiness felt like freedom rather than deprivation.

The chapel doors loomed ahead, massive oak panels bound with iron that had rusted to the colour of dried blood. They were barred not by lock or chain but by tradition more binding than any metal—the unspoken rule that no child left without blessing, no novice without dismissal, no stranger without name or purpose. The wood was carved with scenes from scripture: angels announcing glad tidings, shepherds following stars, the faithful rising from their graves. Tonight those carved figures seemed to watch him with particular attention, as though recognizing a kindred spirit in his transformation.

Yet when he pressed his hand to the wood, feeling the grain beneath his palm like the lines of some enormous fingerprint, the bar lifted with no resistance. The mechanism moved as though oiled by providence itself, as though the chapel were eager to release him from its embrace. Perhaps even buildings could grow weary of their burdens.

Et dimitte nobis debita nostra, sicut et nos dimittimus debitoribus nostris.

Forgiveness—the word hung in the air like incense smoke. But who was forgiving whom? Was he absolving them of their worship, their need to make him into something he had never chosen to become? Or were they, unknowing, releasing him from the debt of gratitude he had never truly owed?

The doors opened with a sound like the world's largest page being turned, and the night air struck his wounds hard—cold, sharp, unsoftened by stone walls or stained glass. It carried the scent of earth and growing things, of rain on leaves and wind across open fields. But despite the pain he drew it in greedily, his lungs aching with the unfamiliar freedom of it, tasting autumn and distance and possibility. Beneath his bandages, his remaining feathers stretched and hummed, responding to this first breath of unfiltered sky since their last feeding, as though remembering what they were meant for.

Et ne nos inducas in tentationem.

But what was temptation now? The urge to stay, to return to safety and certainty? Or the pull of the world beyond these walls, vast and terrifying and utterly without scripture to guide him?

He stepped across the threshold, his feet finding grass instead of stone, earth instead of marble. The sensation was so foreign it nearly made him stumble—the give of soil beneath his weight, the whisper of wind-stirred vegetation around his ankles. Above him stretched a sky punctured with stars, each one a distant sun burning with cold fire. He had seen them through windows, but never felt their light directly on his skin.

Sed libera nos a malo.

The words emerged as barely a whisper, more breath than sound, but they carried across the night like a final benediction. Behind him, the chapel loomed against the darkness, its windows glowing faintly with the light of sanctuary lamps that would burn until dawn. It looked smaller from outside, less imposing—just a building of stone and wood and human ambition, nothing more divine than the will to believe in divinity.

The doors shut behind him with a sound like the last line of a hymn, like the closing of a book whose story had finally reached its end. The echo lingered for a moment, then was absorbed by the vast indifference of the night.

The prayer fell into silence so complete it seemed to swallow itself. For the first time in memory, no bells answered him, no voices rose in response, no footsteps hurried to investigate the sound. There was only wind and starlight and the vast, terrible freedom of being utterly alone and forgotten.

Amen.

CASSETTE 002

[Click.]

[A soft rustle, the whir of the recorder]

I don't think I was meant to talk this much.

I mean—I don't usually. Not out loud. And not to... anyone. But I told myself I'd try to fill a whole cassette before my birthday. One complete thing. Just for me.

[Pauses]

It's strange how many words there are when you're alone. Like they come flooding in just because no one's asking for them. I've filled half my journal and ruined three pens just... talking to paper. Writing to nothing.

And the funny thing is—I still feel like I'm being too loud.

Sometimes I wonder if I was born in the wrong century. Or the wrong body. Or the wrong time. People always say I'm "gifted," but they never mean it kindly. They say it like I've been cursed with the burden of meaning something. As if I must already know what to do with myself.

But I don't. I really don't.

[A longer pause.}

Sister Elira caught me watching the wind today. Said it was "an odd thing to do for someone so clever." But I like watching things that don't speak. They move in their own language. The grass. The birds. The clouds when they roll in like waves and turn the chapel windows gold.

I think that's what I want to be like. Something people don't have to understand. Just... something they sit beside and maybe feel a little better.

[He stutters in uncertainty.]

It's—It's not that I don't want to be known. I do. I just... I don't know if I'm the kind of person people are meant to know.

[Whispers]

I think some people are built to be witnesses. And some are built to be forgotten.

[Pause]

I used to pray to be seen. I used to close my eyes so tight it hurt, and whisper the same thing over and over. "Let someone see me. Let someone remember my name."

But I stopped.

I don't pray anymore. I write. And now I talk. Into this.

[A small smile in his voice]

It's less humiliating.

[He pauses, taking a breath]

I think I'll end this one here.

I'm not sure if I said anything worth keeping.

But it's mine.

And maybe that's enough for tonight.

[Pause.]

Goodnight.

[Click.]

II

CASSETTE 003

[Click.]

[Soft static hum. Errevale breathes in, then out. His voice is a little deeper than the first recording, but still gentle. There's a pause before he begins.]

I think today was the first time I saw something I wasn't supposed to.

Not like in stories. Not angels. Not miracles. Not anything like that. Just… something I don't know how to… process.

[He sighs, shifting.]

It was early. Before dawn. I couldn't sleep again. The dormitory was too warm and I kept dreaming of tapping sounds that didn't stop when I woke up. So… I got up to walk. That's allowed, if you're quiet. The sisters say God doesn't keep office hours.

So I walked. Just down the main corridor. The chapel door was open a little. Not enough to be inviting. Just enough to say someone forgot to close it all the way.

I don't know why I went in. I wasn't planning to pray. I didn't even have shoes on. It felt like sleepwalking.

The candles were out. Moonlight coming through the stained glass made the colours look wrong—green where they should've been red, faces stretched on the floor like melted saints.

And then I saw him.

Father Bell.

At first, I thought he was kneeling in prayer. But… he wasn't praying.

He was crying.

Just—just crying. Into the altar cloth. His shoulders were shaking. His hands were gripping the edge of the table like something might pull him under if he let go.

I didn't say anything. I didn't move.

I've seen people cry before. Children. Pilgrims. Sister Marianne when she burned the Advent bread. I've cried myself, I'm sure. But never him.

He's the one who blesses things. The one who names things. I thought he was made of iron, not... tears.

It felt... I don't know. Like hearing the chapel groan in the night and realizing it's not just old wood—it's hurting.

I backed away before he saw me. I don't think he ever looked up.

I went back to bed and pretended to sleep.

[He breathes quietly. There's a small creak of wood—he may be rocking slightly in a chair.]

All day I kept waiting for someone to say something. Like maybe the sisters would mention that Father Bell wasn't at breakfast. Or that he left a note. But no one said anything. He was at vespers. He read the same verse. He nodded at me in passing.

His eyes looked tired. But not ashamed. Not like someone who broke.

Maybe he doesn't think crying is breaking.

Maybe it's me who thought that.

[He shifts—something soft brushes the mic. He's holding the recorder closer now.]

I don't know why it's stuck in my head. People cry all the time. I know that.

But there's something about it—about him—that makes it feel different.

Like... if he can cry, then everything might be wrong. Not all at once. But just enough that the world tilts a little to one side and doesn't go back.

I always thought faith was supposed to stop that feeling. That belief was like a pillar. Something to lean on when the rest of you trembles.

But what do you do when the pillar trembles too?

I keep remembering the way his hands clutched the cloth. Like maybe he wasn't holding on to something, but holding something in.

And I keep wondering...

What could make a man like that cry into an altar?

Did something happen?

Did he hear something?

Did he stop hearing something?

I think that's what scared me most. Not the crying itself, but the idea that maybe he cried because God didn't answer him.

Or… because he realized He never had.

[He speaks softer now. As if he's closer to the microphone, or to the thought.]

There's a reason I didn't tell anyone.

Because if I do, then it becomes real.

Not just an image.

A fact.

A failure.

A crack in the floor of the place I thought was safe.

And maybe that's what frightened me most—not the sound, not even the sight, but the silence after.

That no one would speak of it. That something so fragile could happen in the holiest room in the house, and still the bells ring, and the prayers go on, and no one looks twice.

Like we all agree not to see it.

And if you're the only one who did... then what are you supposed to do with it?

Carry it?

Or bury it?

[He breathes in sharply—then exhales slowly. Another pause. Then a softer closing tone.]

I'm not angry at Father Bell.
If anything, I feel closer to him.

But I also feel farther from the chapel.

Like it's hollow now, even when it's full of people.

Maybe this is part of growing up.

Maybe faith has to crack a little so you can hear what's behind it.

I don't know. I just needed to say it out loud.

Because I can't forget it.

And if I can't forget it...

Then maybe I was meant to remember.

[A very long pause. The distant sound of bells through a window.]

Goodnight, Father. I hope it helped.

[Click.]

VII

The woods did not want him.

Asael could feel it in the way the branches stooped, lowering their arms like penitents ashamed to be seen with him. He felt it in the moss that squelched cold under his bare feet, drawing away even as it softened. He had thought the world would be larger outside the chapel—that freedom would mean expanse, air, sky—but the forest crowded close, pressing bark against his shoulders, briars against his calves, shadows against the hollow of his throat.

He wrapped himself in the coarse wool of the robe he had stolen from the vestry before leaving. It was too large, the sleeves trailing damp against the leaf-litter. Underneath, his body carried the stains of flight—scratches where branches had clawed him, bruises blooming across his ribs from when he stumbled against roots, the raw and weeping seam of his mouth where his silence had finally given way to opening. The bandages he had tied there were already dyed, speckled dark with blood and down.

He had imagined, once, that the woods would be quieter than the chapel. That its silence would feel like rest, not punishment. But here the silence was alive. Every insect's wings hummed like organs in miniature, every snapping twig cracked like bone, every rustle overhead whispered syllables he half understood. The trees spoke to one another, and he could almost follow. Almost.

He did not want to be followed.

So he hid.

He learned quickly that the best way to vanish was to fold himself small against stone or root and wait. His body knew how to wait. He had been bred for patience in cloisters and cells, trained in the long art of stillness. The sisters had taught him that devotion meant endurance: hold your tongue, hold your breath, hold your body like a prayer pressed too long between palms. In the woods, those same skills made him invisible.

But hiding did not erase the weight in his throat.

It stirred in him at night, when sleep stripped him bare. The first time he dreamed among the trees, he woke choking on feathers. They fanned from his mouth like weeds from tilled soil, small and wet, plastered to his cheeks with saliva and blood. He gathered them in his trembling hands, each downy plume a betrayal, proof of what his body carried. He pressed them into the mud until they vanished, though their outline lingered faintly in the earth like bruises.

In his dreams, the feathers were words.

He dreamed of syllables not yet spoken, sounds that itched and pricked against the scar of his lips. They pressed at him like fledglings battering their wings against the shell of an egg. He woke gagging on them, and when he pressed his fingers against his throat he swore he could feel letters moving beneath the skin.

He began to test them when he thought the night would forgive him. Small sounds, fragments. The hiss of air drawn through teeth, the whisper of a vowel shaped but not voiced. Each one cost him.

A scrape, a cough of blood, a trickle of down that clung to the roots at his feet. He feared to speak louder, to give shape to the whole of a word. Not only because he knew what his voice could do—erase, devour, hollow—but because he did not know if his throat could bear it.

Sometimes the syllables escaped without his will. He would

exhale and the air would catch, twist, split into something half-heard: a consonant fractured, a vowel cut raw. When this happened, the trees around him shivered. The bark darkened with moisture, as though the syllable had left condensation behind. Branches groaned as though they recognized what he carried.

He hated himself for trying.

He knew better.

He had seen what his curse can take.

And still—still—his body itched to make sound. The urge was instinctual, like the compulsion to breathe after drowning.

Language haunted him.[9]

In the chapel, he had written his voice into being. Here, the words wanted to be air again. They ached for shape, for the violence of expulsion. At dusk, as the trees leaned inward and shadows bled into one another, he would sit with his back to a stone outcrop and let them come. His lips parted, trembling. His jaw cracked at its hinges. His tongue feathered and curled, brushing the roof of his mouth. But only the faintest breath escaped, sharp as a blade drawn across parchment.

It was not enough.

He wanted to believe that silence was safer. That to keep himself clamped shut was mercy. But the words inside him burned. They were not passive. They were not holy. They were restless things, pushing against him from within, battering their wings against his flesh until his dreams split with the sound of their beating.

The nights worsened.

---

9   *"I wish I could undo that book sometimes. Is that a sin? To want to undo what you did for God? What if it hurts you to keep?"*

87

When he slept, he dreamed of syllables like swarms. He dreamed of alphabets rotting, of letters with wings gnawing at his ribs, of words carving themselves into the inner walls of his throat. He woke with scratches along his palate, with blood drying at the corner of his lips. He woke tasting iron, the acrid sweetness of decay. His dreams bled into waking so thoroughly he began to fear he would not know the difference when his voice finally broke free.

During the day, he wandered further into the woods, though the branches seemed to bend to mark his passage. He wanted to lose himself, but the trees remembered him. Each step felt traced. Each hiding place grew thinner, as though the forest itself were ashamed of harbouring him.

When he crouched among roots, waiting for the sun to pass, he pressed his nails into the dirt until they split. He scraped at the ground as though burying himself. Sometimes he imagined covering his whole body with soil, letting the forest swallow him, pressing his silence down where it could no longer itch.

But the words would not let him. They curled in his marrow, prickling his dreams, whispering against his teeth. They urged him toward utterance, even as he begged himself to remain quiet. He feared what sound would take from the world if he gave it shape. He feared more what silence was taking from him.

So, he did not speak.

He pressed his mouth shut with blood crusted hands.

He pressed his tongue down with teeth until it ached.

He pressed his silence against the trees until they bent, ashamed.

He hid, but the language inside him did not. It waited, crouched with him in the dark, wings folded too tightly to endure forever.

And when he dreamed again, he knew the feathers would come.

VIII

The forest seemed to speak in absence—whole clearings emptied of song. No sparrows in the brambles, no woodpeckers at their work, no rustle of fox through underbrush. Asael noticed first when he woke to silence too profound, broken only by the stutter of his own breath. He sat upright in the roots where he had curled, robe clinging damp to his skin, and listened. The woods had swallowed their own voice.

When he walked, creatures scattered. Not with the quick dart of prey before a predator, but with reverence, as though a shadow larger than him passed overhead. Deer froze when his figure flickered between trees. They stared, ears trembling, before either bounding away in terror or bowing their necks in some strange submission, antlers catching on branches as if tugged downward by unseen hands. Once, a hare crossed his path and stopped dead still, body taut with fear. Asael extended his hand out of instinct, palm open, but the animal shrieked—a shrill, ragged sound—and bolted into the thickets, leaving tufts of fur caught on thorns.

He thought perhaps he carried death inside him. That animals smelled it in his breath, saw it in the seam of his mouth where feathers bristled against blood. He did not fault them for fleeing. He would have fled himself if he could.

But sometimes they did not flee.

One night, he stumbled upon a stag at the edge of a clearing. Its antlers were vast, burdened with velvet and early moss. The beast did not run. It knelt. Slowly, both legs bending until its chest pressed against the earth, bowing its head as though Asael carried a crown invisible to his own eyes. He felt sick. Sacredness was worse than fear. He whispered a sound—just a vowel, a thin thread of breath—and the stag's ears flicked back. Its body shivered, muscles trembling beneath fur, and when it raised its head again its eyes were clouded, opaque, as though vision itself had been erased. It staggered into the woods, stumbling blindly, crashing against trunks until the sound faded into silence.

He no longer allowed himself to approach any living thing.

By daylight, he gathered scraps. Bark peeled thin from birch, broad leaves torn from ferns, stones flat enough to mark with ash. He wrote the words he remembered from scripture, crooked letters pressed with bloodied fingertips. *Pater. Noster. Sanctus.* The words bled into the grain of wood and leaf, smudging into shapes half ruined before he could finish. When the rain came, his writings melted, inkless prayers dissolving into the mud.

At night, he rehearsed their sound.

Whispers, careful and thin. Consonants shaped in silence before air could charge them with ruin. He mouthed syllables against his arm, pressing lips to fabric to stifle them, feeling his own breath rebound warm and damp against his skin. Still, even the smallest leak of sound warped the air. The grass around him grew brittle, pale as if frost had burned it. Flowers that had been closed against night fell open too quickly, petals wilting in an instant, their softness stripped away until only veins remained.

He wept silently into his sleeve, ashamed. Even practice left wounds.

One evening he wrote the word *mercy* on his palm with soot and stared at it until the black dust smudged into his skin. He tried to say it. Not fully—just the first syllable, a broken "mer". The word came out like the crack of bone. He watched as a moth that had been circling his shoulder fell mid-flight, wings turning to paper ash before it touched the ground. He crushed the fragile body beneath his heel, though it was already ruined beyond recognition.

"Mercy," he mouthed again, this time with no sound, only breath. The silence rang louder than the word itself.

He began to fear that language was not meant for him at all. That letters on bark and whispers in his throat were desecrations, attempts at holiness with a body unfit for scripture. Each utterance seemed to demand a trade; sound for softness, voice for life. He thought of the stag, blinded. The hare, shrieking. The moth, reduced to dust. Was this what he was—a mouth that fed on gentleness until nothing remained?

The forest confirmed his suspicion. It receded from him. Birds no longer sang in the branches he passed under. Small things hid before he came into view. He walked in a silence deeper than the one he carried, a silence imposed upon the world around him.

Sometimes, in the bleakest hours, he pressed his face against the ground and whispered into the soil, hoping his voice would root itself there instead of in the air. But even the earth seemed to wither beneath his breath, worms crawling out of the damp only to writhe blindly on the surface until they stilled. He buried them with shaking hands, palms smeared in dirt and weary gentleness, praying without words that their lives would not count against him.

And yet, he could not stop.

The longing to speak was stronger than hunger, stronger than thirst. It gnawed at him, a need not of the body but of the soul. He wrote the same words over and over, on stones, on bark, on his own skin: *listen, forgive, remember.* Words he feared would never reach anyone without destroying them. He practiced their syllables in the hollow of his chest, shaping them like contraband, half-formed, half-choked.

"I don't hate sainthood. I'm simply... scared of what it means to be holy." Each attempt stole something. A moth, a patch of grass, the

clarity of an animal's eyes. Each failure left him smaller, emptier. He was both the thief and the witness, watching the world unravel thread by thread under the pressure of his tongue.

At times, he thought of returning to the chapel, begging the sisters to bind his mouth shut, to stitch him closed so the hunger could not spill. But he remembered their eyes, wide with fear after his sob, and he knew they would not touch him now. They would leave him gagged and chained, a relic of silence, worshiped only because his voice was hidden.

So he stayed in the forest. Practicing words that ruined the things that heard them, dreaming syllables that left his mouth raw with blood, carving prayers onto his body like wounds. He told himself it was learning and control. That this was the cost of survival. But each morning he woke surrounded by withered grass, ash where insects had been, and feathers scattered like discarded notes, proof that he was a language no one could bear to listen to.

IX

Hunger did not descend all at once but seeped, slow and insistent, into every hollow of his body. At first, Asael mistook it for weariness—his steps heavy, his breath drawn sharp. But as the days stretched, he felt it gnaw deeper, a presence beneath his ribs more constant than breath.

The forest was no refuge. The fruit he found spoiled beneath his fingers, skins collapsing into rot when he touched them. Berries blackened before they reached his lips, seeds shrivelling as if scorched from within. Once, he plucked an apple from a low branch and held it in his palm. By the time he raised it to his mouth, it was already soft with mildew, its flesh grey and weeping. He hurled it against a tree and watched the pulp ooze down bark like pus.

Meat fared no better. When he snared a rabbit in a crude loop of vine, it died too quickly, not by the choke of the cord but by a sudden stillness. Its eyes dulled the instant it looked at him. He opened its body with trembling hands, but the flesh inside was wasted, organs slick and writhing with maggots, bones crumbling into dust. He wept into its fur and buried it beneath a cairn of stones, murmuring no prayer, for fear that words themselves would be another kind of desecration.

Soon, he learned to keep his distance. He touched nothing, tasted nothing. He drank only from streams, though even there he noticed the water growing brackish after he bent to sip. Frogs floated belly-up near the banks, their limbs stiff as if frozen mid-motion. He cupped the water in his hands and drank with his eyes closed, ashamed of the ripples his breath alone could spoil.

Hunger carved him thin. His cheeks hollowed; his robe clung tighter to the angles of his body, stiff with dirt and dried blood. His feathers fell more often now, littering the ground where he slept, brittle as if they too had starved. Each morning he gathered them and buried them, but more appeared, as though his body was unspooling faster than he could contain it.

At night, the dreams returned.

They began with a tickle at the back of his throat, then spread—barbs tearing, feathers stirring, syllables pushing against the sealed seam of his mouth. He dreamed of crying out for bread, for water, for mercy. Each time he opened his mouth, the world around him split apart: trees wilting, rivers bleeding black, animals falling into heaps of bone. He woke with his throat raw, the taste of iron heavy on his tongue, though no word had crossed his lips.

The temptation grew unbearable. Hunger was a knife, pressing closer each day, urging him to release the voice that had once bent stone and unmade memory. If words could ruin, perhaps they could also provide. Perhaps one syllable, loosed carefully, could summon fruit instead of rot, milk instead of ash. He thought of the stag that had knelt to him, blinded but reverent. Wasn't that proof? That his voice was more than ruin—that it was akin to divine?

But shame was louder.

He remembered the girl in the chapel who had forgotten her mind at a single utterance. He remembered the moth that had turned to ash mid-flight, its wings stilled in his breath. He remembered the stag, staggering sightless through trees. To use his voice now, to trade hunger for harm—it would be no different than sacrifice. And he had no right to sacrifice the innocent for his survival.

So he refused.

He bound his mouth again. He tore strips from the hem of his robe, knotting them across his lips, gagging himself until only breath could escape in shallow wheezes. The fabric smelled of sweat and damp earth, stiff with blood from old wounds, but it was a comfort. With his mouth sealed, he could imagine himself harmless again, the danger contained behind cloth.

Yet the shame deepened.

When he stumbled upon pools of water, he saw himself reflected and turned away. His cheeks were bruised with hollows, his eyes fever-bright, his lips cracked where the cloth rubbed them raw. The feathers at his throat were matted, stained, no longer luminous but ragged as a scavenger's. He pressed his hands over his face until darkness smothered the image. He did not want to see the thing that hunger had sculpted him into—a boy thin as bone, a creature halfway between angel and corpse.

Once, in desperation, he pressed his palms together and mouthed a prayer into the folds of his gag. *Give us this day...* The words never reached the air, yet he felt them burning inside, churning like embers in the furnace of his chest. He collapsed in the dirt, trembling, ashamed that even silent prayer felt dangerous, that even voiceless words threatened to wound.

He thought often of the sisters. He imagined them eating in their refectory, bread dipped in broth, cups raised to lips. He remembered the sound of spoons against bowls, the rustle of habits, the murmurs of blessing. He longed for that ordinary rhythm more than the food itself. To eat among others, to be part of a table where silence did not mean exile. But that memory only sharpened the ache inside him.

"Errevale, how is the book coming along?"

He was not meant for tables.

"I have ideas, Father. I'll do my best."

He was meant for wilderness.

"You are a gifted boy, simply let God speak through you. It will come."

For hunger.

For silence that gnawed at both body and soul.

96

Days blurred into nights, nights into days. Time lost its edges. He walked in circles, too weak to keep straight lines, collapsing often beneath trees only to drag himself up again. His ribs jutted like the bars of a cage. His wings, once sharp with strength, now sagged, feathers broken, tips dragging through dirt.

Yet he endured.

Hunger hollowed him, but it did not break him. In that emptiness he carved something harsher than survival: penance. To live without taking, to starve without harm—this became his prayer, his fast, his fragile dignity. If his voice was a curse, then silence was his offering, his sacrifice to a world he could not stop from unravelling at his breath.

Still, the shame did not relent.

When he woke in the mornings, he saw the withered patches of ground where he had slept, grass bent and brittle beneath his body. Even silence left scars. Even stillness ruined. He pressed his forehead to the earth and whispered apologies that no one could hear, gagged words churning hot and damp against cloth.

Perhaps shame itself was the true hunger, he thought. A hunger that could not be satisfied, only deepened. And he would feed it until there was nothing left of him but bones and feathers scattered like prayers that never reached heaven.

X

The forest had grown accustomed to him, or perhaps he to it. Days stretched into weeks, marked not by bells or prayers but by the rhythm of his hunger, the shuffle of his weakened steps, the slow fall of feathers trailing behind him like breadcrumbs.

He had almost convinced himself he was invisible. A shadow that passed through thickets without trace, a hush that bled into the hush of the trees. When he crossed streams, he scattered no fish. When he brushed against brambles, they wilted rather than clung. The woods did not resist him, but neither did they welcome him. He was tolerated, like a scar tolerated by the body it marred.

Until the day the hermit saw him.

It was evening, and the air smelled of smoke. Asael followed it without thinking—an old instinct, carried from years of cloister fires and cooking hearths. The scent promised warmth, or at least the ghost of food. His body shook as he stumbled toward it, knees grazing roots, palms raw where he caught himself against bark.

The clearing opened, a space ringed by oaks and marked with a stone hearth at its centre. A small hut leaned crooked against the trees, its walls of rough-hewn timber patched with hides. Smoke leaked from a hole in the roof. A figure hunched near the fire, muttering in a low, steady rhythm.

Asael froze.

The man was old—beard wild, hair bound in a knotted strip of cloth. His robe was tattered, patched with bits of fur and rough stitching. A rosary hung from his neck, beads worn smooth from years of thumb and breath. His hands trembled as he fed kindling into the flames, but his eyes, when they lifted, were sharp.

They found Asael immediately.[10]

He tried to retreat into shadow, but his body betrayed him. A dry cough tore from his chest, feathers catching in his throat. His gag, loosened with days of wear, slipped down around his neck, exposing cracked lips and the crooked seam of his mouth. He staggered against a tree, pale down spilling from his lips and scattered wet at his feet to the forest floor.

The hermit gasped.

"Angel."

It wasn't a question, more so said as if stating fact. As if creating a reality Asael had no say in.

Asael shook his head violently, stumbling backward. His wings trembled, bones jutting through thin skin, feathers ragged. He wanted to vanish, to melt into bark and earth, but the word clung to him, heavy as chains.

The hermit rose unsteadily, clutching his rosary. "Angel," he said again, louder this time, with awe that fractured into fear. His knees bent, and he fell to the ground in a clumsy kneel. The firelight painted his face orange, his tears silver. "God preserve me... I see you. I see You."

Asael's stomach twisted. He pressed trembling hands over his mouth, as if to seal in the syllables trying to rise. Not angel. Not holy. Not seen.

He wanted to scream it, but silence was safer. Silence was

---

10   *"There's something following me. It doesn't walk. It doesn't breathe. It doesn't wait. But it knows when I'm alone."*

less ruinous than truth.

But the hermit would not relent.

He began to chant, half prayer, half ecstasy. Snatches of psalms and invocations tumbling from his lips, words tripping over each other. "Sanctus, sanctus—Lord of hosts—divine messenger, God's own winged child—" His voice cracked, but he continued, desperate, as if his words could sanctify the broken thing crouched before him.

The shame burned hotter than hunger.

To be called angel was to be recognized. To be recognized was to be fixed in place, no longer shadow, no longer free to dissolve.

Recognition was prison.

He stumbled forward, shaking his head so violently his vision blurred. He wanted to plead. *I am not what you name me!* But even gagless, he dared not open his mouth. He knew what one word could do.

Still, the hermit's eyes shone with reverence. He stretched out his arms as though to embrace. "Speak," he begged, voice cracking with tears. "Oh, angel, speak to me. Bless me. I am unworthy, but speak."

The syllables clawed inside Asael's throat. Not prayer, not blessing—something rawer, heavier, desperate. Hunger urged him: speak, and the fire will not devour; speak, and food will come; speak, and shame will scatter. The feathers in his throat quivered, greedy for what it desired to claim for offering.

But shame crushed him down. He fell to his knees, gag clutched in his hands, and pressed it back against his lips until blood seeped from cracks reopened. He shook his head, tears streaking his face, throat convulsing angrily against the restraint.

The hermit did not understand. He mistook refusal for humility. "Yes," he whispered, lowering his head to the earth. "Too holy to answer. Too merciful for words. Forgive me, forgive my asking."

And with that, he prostrated fully, his forehead pressed to the dirt at Asael's feet. His back bent like a bow, hands outstretched in worship.

And Asael could not breathe.

He had left the chapel to escape this very gaze. He had starved himself to deny this very hunger—for witness, for reverence, for destruction. And yet here it was, kneeling before him, calling him what he feared most. Angel.

The fire cracked.

Smoke curled.

The hermit wept into the earth.

So he fled.

He ran blindly into the trees, branches tearing his arms, feet stumbling through roots. His gag slipped loose, but he held his mouth shut, jaw aching from the effort. The word chased him— *angel, angel, ANGEL*—clinging to his bones, burning his muscles and nerves and organs until they boiled within him.

When he finally collapsed against a fallen trunk, chest heaving, he clawed at his skin as though he could tear the name free. Feathers scattered, blood streaked his arms, his ribs jutted sharp as knives.

Still, he whispered nothing.

Silence was his only defence, his only prayer. But silence had failed him once again.

He had been seen.

And in being seen, he had been named.

XI

He dreamed of the chapel again.

Not the chapel as it was, but as it might have been if silence had grown into walls, if stillness had calcified into columns and arches that bore the weight of unuttered prayers.[11] Everything was pale, pale, pale—white stone bleached of colour and warmth, white candles that burned without flame, white light filtering through windows that showed no saints, no martyrs, no stories of suffering transformed to glory. Only blank glass, smooth as ice, reflecting nothing back to him. Even the crucifix was faceless, a body of marble without eyes or mouth, arms outstretched in mute surrender to a silence that had swallowed even its own name.

The air itself seemed thick as honey, pressing against his ears until they rang with emptiness. His footsteps made no noise against the stone floor, though he could feel the cold seeping through his bare soles, spreading up through his bones like winter taking root.

He stood before the altar barefoot, his gown torn at the hem where thorns had caught it, or perhaps where his own desperate hands had clawed at the fabric in some half remembered panic. The feathers that lined his throat were visible even from a distance, bristling like thorns from the seam of his mouth, dark against his pale skin. They rustled when he breathed, restless, hungry, pressing outward as though seeking escape from the prison of his flesh. Each breath made them shiver and dance, a living constellation of want mapped across his throat.

---

11   *"I keep dreaming of the chapel's ceiling collapsing in. I always wake before it does."*

The altar stretched before him, vast and white as bone, carved from a single piece of stone that seemed to glow with its own internal light. Upon its surface, a spool of silk appeared as if conjured from prayer itself—golden, glimmering faintly, impossibly smooth. The thread caught the strange chapel light and threw it back in ribbons of amber and honey. Its surface was perfect and unmarred, beautiful in the way that sacred things were beautiful.

It unrolled toward him as though of its own accord, trailing across the altar's edge and down toward the floor, a golden river that whispered against stone as it moved. It pooled briefly at the base of the altar before stretching further, crossing the cold floor until it brushed the tops of his feet like a benediction, warm and alive against his skin.

He bent to pick it up, his movements slow and deliberate as though he were performing a ritual he had practiced in dreams for years. The thread was lighter than air between his fingers, yet substantial, real in a way that the rest of the dream chapel was not.

The silk was warm. It pulsed faintly beneath his touch, as if blood ran through its golden fibres. As if it were not thread at all but something living, something that had once carried life through veins and arteries. He could feel its rhythm against his palm—steady and patient.

A needle rested beside the spool, long and silver, gleaming like a sliver of bone pulled from some celestial ribcage. Its point was sharp enough to pierce flesh, to part skin like water, to draw forth the crimson offerings that dreams demanded. He knew what was expected of him, though no voice told him. No hand guided him. No scripture instructed his movements. This knowledge came from somewhere deeper than teaching, older than words. This was instinct, or prophecy, or both—the understanding written into his bones before birth.

His hands moved without trembling, a certainty that

belonged to the dream rather than to him. He lifted the needle, its weight familiar in his palm though he had never held its like. The silver was cold against his skin, but the cold was welcome, bracing, like the touch of winter air on fevered flesh.

He threaded the needle with careful precision, watching as the golden silk slipped through the eye with liquid ease. The thread seemed to sing as it passed through, a note too high for human hearing but felt in the marrow of his bones. And brought the point to his lips.

The first puncture was baptism, sharp and clean and holy. A bead of blood welled on his lower lip, scarlet against pale flesh, perfect as a ruby caught in candlelight. The metallic taste flooded his mouth, copper and salt mixing with something oddly sweet. The thread slid through the wound, tugging the skin tight, drawing his flesh together.

Another puncture followed, deliberate and sure.

Then another.

Each one a prayer without words, each knot a denial of sound, each stitch a small death that brought him closer to the silence he craved.

He sewed carefully, deliberately, as if binding a book whose pages must never be read, whose words must never be spoken aloud. His fingers worked with the practiced grace of a seamstress, though he had never learned such skills in waking life.

The needle pierced and withdrew, pierced and withdrew, creating a rhythm that matched the beating of his heart, the distant thunder of wings that might have been his own.

Finally, his lips sealed, his mouth vanishing beneath the golden thread as though it had never existed. Only a neat line of gold crossed his face, glistening faintly in the blank chapel light, beautiful and terrible and final. The stitches were perfect and even, tight enough to hold against any attempt at speech but loose enough to allow the shallow breathing that would keep his body alive while his voice died in his throat.

The feathers inside thrashed against this new prison, desperate to escape, beating against the walls of his flesh like caged birds. But the thread held fast, sanctified by dream logic, made strong by the weight of symbols he did not fully understand. His chest rose and fell with strangled breaths that whistled faintly through his nose. Every inhale was a struggle, each exhale a small surrender.

The marble Christ above him began to weep—not tears of saltwater, but of molten gold that dripped slowly from its carved eyes. Liquid metal fell onto his shoulders, searing his skin like wax, marking him with burns that would heal into scars shaped like halos and wings. The pain was purifying, the kind of suffering that saints wrote about in their hidden journals.

And then—he woke.

The dream dissolved like smoke in wind but the ache remained, deeper now, feeling more real than the waking world that surrounded him. His cheeks throbbed with remembered pain. He touched them with trembling fingers and found faint grooves pressed into his flesh, as if thread had indeed pierced the skin, and the needle's passage had left its mark in the territory between sleep and waking. Fine lines marked the corners of his mouth, red and swollen, tender to the touch. When he swallowed, the taste of silk lingered bitter on his tongue—metallic and faintly sweet.

He sat up slowly in the hollow of his makeshift shelter, his body ached from sleeping on the hard ground and the cold that had seeped through his thin clothing to his bones. His breath fogged in the morning air, the forest dim with the grey half-light of dawn. The world smelled of damp earth and dying leaves, the slow decay that marked autumn's passage into winter.

Around him, scattered like evidence of some celestial violence, feathers littered the ground in drifts that caught the pale light and threw it back in ripples of white and silver. They lay thick as snowfall, marking every place his body had touched the earth during his restless sleep. His trail was obvious, unmistakable—a line of white leading back through the trees like breadcrumbs in a children's tale, betraying his every movement to any who might seek to follow.

Shame flushed through him, hot and immediate, rising from his chest to colour his cheeks with the heat of exposure. The hermit's voice echoed in his memory like a prophecy he could not escape— *angel, angel, angel.* The word still burned in his ears, syllables that carried the weight of recognition, of naming, of being seen when he had tried so desperately to become invisible. To be named was to be reclaimed. To be dragged back into the light he had fled. And to be found was to be ruined, reduced to symbol and story, transformed from person into parable.

He could not allow it.

He *would* not allow it.

He rose on unsteady legs, weak from hunger and cold but resolute in his purpose. His hands shook as he began to gather the feathers, cradling them as if they were fallen birds, as if each white plume were a small life that deserved gentle handling even in death. He hated them. Hated how gingerly he treated them, hated what they had turned him into. He carried them in careful armfuls to the stream that ran near his shelter, its water dark and quick-moving, fed by mountain springs that had never known the touch of human hands.

One by one, he cast the blasphemous feathers into the current, watching as the water caught them and carried them away, spinning them in small eddies before drawing them downstream toward places he would never see. The white plumes looked like stars scattered across the dark water, beautiful and doomed as they disappeared around the bend where the stream curved away into deeper forest. He wished he could do the same to himself.

And he debated it.

What would happen if he cast his own body into the current? If he allowed himself to destroy himself the way his throat destroyed those near him?

But alas he didn't, his legs shaking too hard at the thought and he hated himself for that much more. The audacity to want to live, to survive.

When the last feather had vanished from sight, he turned his attention to the ground itself. He scoured the earth where he had lain, dragging stones across the packed soil to break the imprint his body had left during the long night. The work was hard, his muscles screaming protest with each movement, but he persisted with the desperate energy of the hunted. He smeared ash from an old fire over tree bark where his blood had dried in rusty stains, grinding the char into the wounds until they disappeared beneath dark smudges that could have been anything—storm damage, lightning strikes, the natural weathering of wood exposed to wind and rain.

He worked for hours as the sun climbed higher, undoing every trace of his passage through this place. Every sign of himself was hunted down and destroyed with methodical precision. He tore down branches that had bent beneath his weight, snapping them cleanly so they would appear to have been broken by wind. He trampled grass to make it seem unmarked by any human foot, scattered leaves to bury the faint outlines where his bare soles had pressed into soft earth. Where his tears had fallen, he poured stream water until the salt was washed away, until the ground held no memory of his grief.

The forest grew restless under his frantic ministrations. Birds shrieked alarm calls and fled their perches, wings beating frantically as they sought the safety of deeper woods. A fox that had been watching from the undergrowth crouched low and bolted, red tail flashing between the trees like a tongue of flame. Even the trees seemed to recoil from his touch, as though insulted by his violent denial of presence and his refusal to accept his place in the natural order of things.

But Asael persisted, driven by a fear deeper than exhaustion, stronger than hunger or cold. His movements grew more desperate as the day wore on, his breathing harsh and ragged as he fought to erase every molecule of himself from the forest's memory. Sweat stung his eyes despite the autumn chill, and his hands bled from rough stone and broken bark, but still he worked.

By dusk, when the first bats began to stir in the deepening shadows, nothing remained of his presence. No feather marked his passage. No stain told the story of his tears. No impression in the earth held the shape of his sleeping form. The clearing looked as though no human foot had ever disturbed its peace, as though the forest had reclaimed even the memory of his existence.

The world no longer remembered him, and that forgetting was exactly what he had sought.

He collapsed against a boulder, chest heaving, throat raw from the silent sobs that had wracked his body throughout the long day of erasure. His lips burned where dreamed thread had cut them, the phantom pain as real as any wound carved by waking steel. He pressed his sleeve to his mouth until the trembling stopped, until the urge to cry out his anguish to the uncaring sky finally passed.

For the first time, in the settling quiet of twilight, he realized the full weight of what he had done. Not just hidden himself, but erased himself entirely. He was becoming less than shadow and less than silence, not even the space between heartbeats. He had become nothing at all, a hole in the world shaped like a boy but containing only emptiness.

And yet... relief flooded through him, sweet as honey and pure as stream water.

There was relief in vanishing, in slipping through the cracks between seen and unseen.

Relief in his own unmaking, in taking apart the story others insisted on writing around him.

Relief in undoing what others insisted on naming and transforming into something that served their needs rather than his own.

The hermit would search and find nothing but an empty forest and his own delusions. The chapel would remember only blood and feathers and the absence where a boy had been. The forest, if it could speak, would say with perfect honesty; there was no one here. No angel passed this way. No miracle walked among these trees.

He tipped his head back against the stone, staring at the sky where the first stars pierced the gathering dark like silver needles through dark cloth. The constellations wheeled overhead in their ancient patterns, indifferent to his struggles, eternal in their silence. They had watched the rise and fall of kingdoms, the birth and death of gods, the coming and going of countless souls who thought themselves important enough to be remembered. Against their vast perspective, his small erasure seemed almost insignificant.

He smiled. Insignificant. His chest puffed out with a small sense of self-loathing pride. He was insignificant.

His voice itched in his throat, a familiar pressure that demanded release, that begged for the freedom of sound and breath and meaning. The urge to break the silence that had become his prison rose like bile in his chest, but he pressed his mouth shut tighter.

Tighter.

Tighter, imagining the golden silk pulling across his lips again, feeling the phantom needle pierce his flesh. He would not speak. He would never speak. Not if it meant being seen, being dragged back into the light that burned rather than blessed.

Better to vanish completely. To unmake himself so thoroughly that even memory could not find him. Better to be nothing than to be the wrong kind of something in other people's stories.

He closed his eyes against the star-scattered darkness, and for the first time in weeks, sleep came without dreams—deep, black, empty sleep that held no chapels, no needles, no golden thread. Just the blessed absence of everything, the perfect silence he had been seeking all along.

Cassette 004

[Click.]

[Soft static hum. A long pause. He doesn't speak immediately. When he does, he sounds distant.]

I think I understand now. It's not really me they want.

They want the boy from the book. They want the miracle child. The quiet thing that says clever, quiet things and doesn't ask to be understood.

They smile at me like I'm an achievement. A relic. Not a person. Not a person who might be hurting.

[He adjusts the recorder slightly, fabric brushing the mic.]

It's strange. You spend your whole life wanting to be seen. Then someone finally looks, and it's worse.

Because they don't see you. They see something useful.

A symbol of some sort of... saviour. A story they can tell about you that never once includes your voice.

[He clears his throat quietly.]

I sat in the old chapel alcove today—the one with the flaking arch and the hymnals no one uses. A younger boy walked past, the one I used to help read. He didn't stop. He looked at me the way you look at a stone. Not with cruelty. Just with… nothing.

And I thought, maybe that's better. Better to be forgotten than to be remembered wrong.

[A pause. There's a long silence, then the click of his tongue against the roof of his mouth, softly.]

Sometimes I wonder if people knew me before I wrote that book. Or if that was the only thing they ever learned about me.

Like I put myself in the pages, and everything left behind just kind of… stopped growing.

No one asks what I'm working on now. No one asks if I'm okay.

They say, "You are so gifted." "You must be proud." "Your parents would've been proud, too."

I think the worst part is that I want to be proud. I just don't remember what it cost me.

There's a painting in the dormitory hallway of the archangel Gabriel.

He's got that same blank look they all have. Stern. Distant. Clean. But today I noticed something. His hands are bleeding.

Not like stigmata. Not holy. Just ripped. Torn open at the palms.

I think that's the part they cropped in the prints.

[Another long pause—he takes a breath, deeper now.]

I think people want the story. Not the voice that told it.

They want the hymn, not the lungs. The art, not the ache. The candlelight, not the burn.

Maybe that's why I've stopped going to choir. Maybe I'm afraid they'll remember my voice wrong and carry it with them anyway.

[He shifts again—fabric rustling. His voice is soft now, but firm.]

I don't know who I am anymore when no one's watching. I'm trying to find out. I've gotten a bit taller, but I don't quite know what else has grown yet. So I'm trying to learn.

To learn me.

But it's hard when everyone keeps looking and expecting the same shape.

If I scream, will they say "he's broken?" If I disappear, will they say "he's fading?"

What if I'm just changing?

Would that be allowed?

[A small breath, almost a laugh, something akin to bitter.]

Maybe I'll write something else. Something they won't understand. Something just for me.

Maybe I already have.

[The tape hums a moment.]

I don't know what they see when you look at me. But I hope, someday, they'll hear what I meant.

[A long pause.]

Goodnight.

[Click.]

III

Cassette 005

[Click]

[Faint rustling. Distant rain. His voice is calm, but thinner than before. Something hollow sits behind each sentence.]

I've started to notice something about the way they speak to me now.

They say things like: "You have a gift."

"You're a light in dark times."

"You're not like the others."

They think they're praising me.

But every word sounds like they're building something around me. Not for me.

Like I'm being wrapped in glass.

[He pauses. The sound of a chair creaking as he shifts his weight.]

Sister Alena called me "a vessel."

She said it like a blessing—like I was lucky to be empty enough for God to fill.

I wanted to ask her, what happens when the vessel wants to keep something of its own?

What happens when the water inside has a name?

…They've stopped asking me how I'm feeling.

They only ask what I'm writing. Or worse—what I've seen.

Like I'm a prophet now.

Or a mirror.

Or a door.

They call it reverence.

But it feels more like… containment.

[He breathes in. The tape hums.]

Today at vespers, they made me sit in front.

Said it was symbolic. That it would "inspire the younger boys."

I didn't want to.

But I couldn't say no. Not anymore.

So I sat there, in that velvet chair, with everyone staring at me like I was some sort of relic.

One of them tried to touch my shoulder as I left.

He whispered, "Thank you for still being here."

I smiled. But something inside me cracked.

[He pauses.]

I used to think I wanted to be seen.

But this isn't seeing. This is… believing in an idea. Not a person.

They're not looking at me.

They're looking at what they think I am.

And the more they believe, the less of me there is left.

[Soft static. Something in the background—perhaps thunder far off.]

I looked at my reflection today.

Not out of vanity. Just… to check.

And I couldn't tell if it looked like me anymore.

The eyes were the same colour.

The hair curled at the ends like always.

But it felt like I was watching someone play me.

A very good actor in very good skin.

I raised my hand to the glass.

And for a moment, I didn't feel anything on the other side.

[He speaks softer now. The rain has stopped. The silence is heavy.]

Do you know what they call saints who are still alive?

Nothing.

There isn't a word for it.

Because it's not supposed to happen.

You're not supposed to be holy while breathing.

Maybe that's why I feel like I'm floating just above the floor.

Like if I took a step too fast, my feet wouldn't find anything solid.

Because holy things don't touch the ground.

Holy things only hover.

And bleed.

And vanish.

[He exhales shakily. Then a pause.]

I think I'm being loved in the wrong shape.

And I don't know how to change back.

[Long silence. Then—very faintly;]

Goodnight.

[Click.]

XII

The woods had grown quieter around him.

Days passed without the sound of birdcall, as though the trees themselves were learning his silence. The underbrush no longer rustled when he walked and the streams no longer rippled at his presence. He thought, for a time, that he had succeeded in becoming invisible.

But hunger betrayed him.

His body thinned. His skin clung too close to bone, pale as wax, and his wings lost their sheen, feathers clumping together like wet ash. He dreamed of bread but woke with his mouth full of feathers, choking them out onto the moss where they clung like guilty confessions.

It was in this state that he stumbled toward the faint glow of lanterns at the forest's edge.

He did not mean to seek them. His feet carried him without thought, driven by the scent of smoke and the thin promise of warmth. It was dusk, and the world was turning violet at the edges, shadows lengthening until they threatened to erase him.

Through the branches, he glimpsed the outline of a chapel— small, weather-worn, its steeple leaning. Its bells had long since cracked; only the hollow space remained. Candles flickered inside, pale halos against stone walls.

He should have fled.

But he was cold. And he was starving.

Asael noticed a nearby clothing line, and crossing himself for forgiveness grabbed a thin cloak and slipped it on. The material scratched at his feathers, but it provided some semblance of warmth. He pressed the hood low over his brow and slipped inside.

The chapel smelled of old wood and wet wool. A few women knelt near the altar, whispering prayers for their dead. A child drowsed against his mother's shoulder. An elder tended to the candles, snuffing those that had burned too low and lighting fresh ones. No one noticed him at first, thin shadow that he was, pale robes hanging loose around his body.

He found a corner in the back and crouched there, hiding his wings beneath his cloak, folding his hunger into silence. He wanted only to rest for a moment, to gather strength before disappearing again.

But then—one of the women looked up.

Her eyes, weary with grief, widened as they fixed on him. He was small and matted, but the feathers that clung to his skin were undeniable and offensive. She clutched the rosary around her neck, lips parting. At first he thought she would scream. But instead, tears filled her eyes, and she whispered, "Blessed Mother... you have sent me an angel."

Her words rippled outward like a stone dropped into water. Heads turned. The air thickened.

The others followed her gaze, and one by one, their expressions shifted—fear first, then awe, then something Asael could not define. A man dropped to his knees.

A child gasped.

The elder crossed himself three times, voice trembling as he began to murmur *Ave Maria, gratia plena...*

Asael's throat tightened.

He pressed himself back into the corner, wishing the stone would swallow him. But their eyes were fixed, and their whispers grew louder. "A sign." "A miracle." "A vessel of *God.*"

The grieving woman rose, trembling, and took a step toward him. Her hands shook as she reached into her satchel and drew out a piece of bread, coarse and dark. She placed it gently on the floor before him, as though laying an offering at an altar.

He stared at it. His stomach cramped with longing, but he could not move, his shame and fear pinning him in place.

Another joined her—a man who set a coin beside the bread, bowing his head as he backed away. Then another, with a sprig of rosemary, then another, with a lock of hair tied in ribbon. Small, ordinary things transformed by intention into gifts for him.

The space around him became an altar.

He wanted to scream. *I am not what you think I am! I am not holy! I am not SAFE!*

But his mouth stayed shut, gag pressing into his teeth, threads of dream-silk still etched into his skin.

The child stirred then, slipping from his mother's lap. He toddled forward, unafraid, and reached out a small hand toward Asael's cloak.

The entire chapel held its breath.

Asael flinched back, wings twitching beneath fabric. He could not bear to be touched, to be confirmed as flesh when they wanted spirit. But he was too weak to stop the child's hand from brushing the edge of his sleeve.

And in that instant—the congregation gasped.

The child's eyes widened, and he smiled, though he did not know why. "Thank you," he whispered, though he had not been given anything. His mother burst into tears and clutched him to her chest, crying that he had been healed, though of what, no one said.

The murmurs rose into fervour. "A blessing!"

"A wonder!"

"God is with us!"

They fell to their knees, the entire chapel bowing as though before the Lord himself. The air vibrated with prayer, voices overlapping in desperate gratitude.

Asael shrank into the corner, trembling, his mouth bleeding where he bit it shut.

For the first time since leaving the cloister, he realized something worse than being forgotten.

To be remembered wrongly.

The prayers would not stop.

They overlapped and tangled, falling into strange rhythms that sounded less like devotion and more like a surging ocean crashing against stone. Latin blurred into dialect, dialect into wordless hums. The women beat their chests with trembling fists. The men pressed their foreheads to the floor.

And Asael—Asael sat trapped in their gaze, his body no longer his own.

The bread lay at his feet, broken open by the child's hand, crumbs scattered like relic dust. The smell of it clawed at his hunger. His stomach convulsed, but he dared not reach for it, dared not feed. To eat in front of them would be to accept divinity, and to accept what they thought he was.

A vessel. The sign of a miracle.

The word pressed against the inside of his throat, but he could not form it. His mouth, half healed from the dream stitches, pulsed with its own heartbeat. The threads had left faint grooves down his cheeks, silver ridges that glistened in the lamplight. They must have looked like stigmata to them—holy marks, not scars.

A door creaked.

The chapel hushed as a figure entered—black cassock, rosary swinging.

The village priest.

His face was narrow, his eyes sunken from years of hearing grief poured into his ears. He froze when he saw the boy in the corner, the kneeling crowd, the scattered offerings.

A beat passed. Then he crossed himself and whispered, "Deus meus."

The congregation surged toward him, voices breaking over one another—"Father, an angel!" "He touched the child!" "A sign from heaven!" Their hands clutched at his sleeves, their tears wetting his cassock.

The priest steadied himself, then approached Asael slowly, as though drawing near to a burning lamp.

"What is your name?" he asked.

Asael lowered his head. His hood shadowed his face. His lips trembled but did not part.

The priest waited. When no answer came, he gestured to the congregation. "Do you not see? He is mute. As angels often are, for their language is not ours."

The crowd murmured agreement, relief. They wanted

holiness, not humanity.

His silence became nothing less than proof.

The priest knelt then, the first among them to lower himself to Asael's level. He took the boy's thin hand—fingers cold, joints sharp—and pressed it to his forehead. Asael tried to pull back, but the priest gripped tighter, whispering words meant for prayer but sounding more like chains.

"There's a new priest. He watches me without shame. It scares me. He says I was born of God's womb to become His voice. That scared me too." "Benedicite. Bless us, holy one." The boy's stomach clenched. His throat fluttered. He wanted to scream *I am no blessing*! But when he tried to form the words, only a dry hiss escaped, feathers rasping against his windpipe.

The priest trembled. He mistook it for grace.

"Do you see?" he cried to the congregation, rising to his feet. "God has sent us a living relic. A vessel for His voice!"

The crowd erupted, hands reaching toward Asael but never touching, their reverence sharper than fear. Some laid more offerings at his feet—rings, beads, coins, hair, scraps of cloth. One woman pressed her bleeding palm to the floorboards before him, leaving a red handprint as though sealing a covenant.

The priest's voice grew louder, more certain. "We shall keep him safe here. Guard him. Feed him. Tend him as we would the Eucharist itself. This boy—this angel—shall not be forsaken."

Safe. Guarded.

The words sank into Asael like stones tied to his ribs. He was not being offered safety but containment.

Not freedom, but a reliquary.

But through his fear, hunger had finally betrayed him.

He reached for the bread. His hand shook, fingers curling around the crust. He lifted it to his mouth, allowing the tattered gag to slip to the floor and tore a piece free with his teeth.

The room gasped.

It was not the act of eating that startled them, but the way his mouth opened—too wide, lips split raw at the corners, teeth too sharp, tongue feathered and pale. They saw what he truly was, if only for an instant.

But they did not scream.

They bowed deeper.

A holiness so grotesque it could only be divine. A horror so intimate it must have been sanctified.

The priest's eyes gleamed. "Do you see? He feeds as we do, yet not as we do! Flesh veils him, yet he is not flesh! He is mystery!"

Mystery. The word that justified anything.

Asael chewed slowly at first, each bite tasting of ash and copper. Shame burned hotter than hunger, but he swallowed anyway. To leave the bread untouched would have been worse—to starve before their eyes was to invite their pity. Better to consume, even if it condemned him.

So he did, his bites becoming greedier. More desperate. Hunger clawed at his stomach, the feathers in his throat pleased to devour even more than memory.

When the bread was gone, silence settled. All eyes fixed on him, waiting for a word. Some sort of gesture or a miracle.

He lowered his head and folded his wings tighter beneath his cloak. His silence hardened.

The priest mistook it for humility.

"He shall stay in the sacristy tonight," he declared. "Tomorrow, we will prepare a space for him. A cell of honour, a reliquary for the living fit for the holy."

The congregation murmured agreement. The women wept softly. The men whispered prayers of gratitude. The child, still clinging to his mother, pointed at Asael and said, "He smiled at me."

Asael had not smiled.

But no one questioned the child.

They wanted to believe. And belief was heavier than truth.

The priest gestured, and two men stepped forward. They did not touch Asael directly—no, they would not dare—but they flanked him, guiding him with the weight of their presence, their arms stretched out as though to create a corridor through the crowd.

"Come," the priest urged gently, like coaxing a skittish lamb. "You will be safe with us."

Safe. That word again. But he knew better To be safe meant to be hidden and bound.

Asael did not rise at first. His body clung to the corner like a shadow. He thought of the trees, the hush of leaves, the silence of the forest. He thought of hunger, and how it was still better than this.

But then a hand reached out—not toward him, but toward the breadcrumbs at his feet. A woman scooped one up, pressed it to her lips, and swallowed.

Her eyes rolled back. She whispered, "Grace."

The crowd stirred. More hands stretched toward the floorboards, seeking fragments of what he had touched, what he had eaten. Their devotion clawed at him more than their fear ever had.

Asael stood.

Gasps rippled like wind through wheat. His hood slipped back just enough to show the thread-marks on his cheek, glinting faintly in the lamplight. The congregation sighed, a sound almost erotic in its surrender.

He lowered his head, wings tucked so tightly they bruised his ribs. The two men walked beside him, though their eyes never left the floor. The priest led, carrying a candle high as though escorting something holy to its shrine.

The chapel air changed.

No longer prayers, no longer hymns—just silence, thick and reverent. Every step Asael took seemed to ring louder than bells, as though his soles pressed not stone but some vast hollow beneath the earth. His shame grew heavier with each echo.

They entered the sacristy.

The room was small, lined with shelves of vestments, chalices, and censers. Shadows clung to the corners, broken only by the candle's glow. The priest turned, his face alight with triumph.

"Here," he said softly, "you will rest tonight. Tomorrow, the bishop must hear of you. He will know what to call you, how best to keep you."

Asael flinched at the word *keep*.

The priest did not notice. He placed the candle on a small table, bowed once, and stepped back. The others followed. No locks, no chains—only the heavier binding of reverence. The door closed with a hollow thud.

Alone, Asael sank to the floor.

The air stank of incense and old wine, of wood polish and smoke. He pressed his hands over his mouth, as though he could seal himself again, praying in hopes that flesh might stitch itself closed if pressed hard enough. His chest heaved. No sound escaped.

He caught sight of himself in the silver of a chalice.

For an instant, he thought it was someone else—a pale boy with hollow eyes, thread-marks carved into his skin, feathers twitching beneath cloth. A figure half-dissolved, blurred between voice and body.

He touched the metal, trembling. The reflection did not move with him.

A fissure split in his mind: the boy, the vessel, the angel, the silence. Which one was he? Which one had they seen? Which one was being buried alive in glass?

A sound escaped him then—not a sob, not a word, just a thin rush of air carrying feathers into his throat. It fogged the chalice, warped the reflection. His face disappeared.

He pressed harder, until the silver bent faintly beneath his touch, until he could almost believe he had been erased.

Outside, the congregation still prayed. Their voices swelled and broke, pleading not with God but with him.

And in the sacristy's dim silence, Asael realized he would never be unseen again.

XIII

The morning bells called him from uneasy sleep. Their toll had always rung through the hills with a clarity that steadied him once, but now the sound clung to his skin like oil, seeping into the hollows of his body.

When he opened his eyes, he knew something waited for him. He had felt it even in the dark—an expectation pressing at his chest like a stone.

The priest came at dawn. Not the same one who had given him shelter when he left the chapel, but a local steward of the parish whose robes smelled faintly of woodsmoke. His face was kind in shape, but not in gaze. He looked at Asael the way one looks at a candle during storm winds: with anxious reverence, fearful of losing the light.

"Come," the priest said, voice careful. "It is vespers. You will sit with us today. In front."

Asael wanted to resist. The words rose at the back of his throat, sharp and winged, but he swallowed them before they could wound anyone. His silence was mistaken for obedience.

The chapel was small, no larger than the refectory he once knew, but it felt cavernous with the crowd gathered inside. He did not know so many had lived in the valley.

Faces pressed into pews, bodies swaying under the wax drip of candles. The air smelled of wet wool and smoke and a faint sweetness he could not name.

The velvet chair sat at the altar's base. It was not ornate, not gilded or jewelled, but its strangeness came from placement. It had no right to be there. It felt too domestic, too human for the solemn stone. Yet it gleamed in the candlelight like a throne awaiting coronation.

The priest gestured, and Asael's feet carried him forward before his will could stop them. Each step rang too loudly on the stone floor. The villagers leaned in, craning necks to see.

When he sat, the velvet kissed the back of his legs with softness that felt more akin to entrapment. The chair swallowed him whole.

Around him, candles were lit. Not just on the altar, but in a widening circle, until the flame-wreath hemmed him in. Their light made the velvet bleed red against his pale body, a smear of sanctity he could not scrub away.

The prayers began.

Low voices rose and fell, and though the words were the same liturgies he had known in childhood, they felt altered, warped by proximity.

They were not directed upward, toward the rafters or heaven.[12]

They were directed at him.

He tried not to look at them, but he could not help it. Their eyes burned against his skin. He had thought himself invisible once, hidden in corners and shadows, but here there was no place to hide. He was laid bare.

---

12   *"The ink smells like blood today. Maybe it always did. Weird that I recognize the scent."*

And it was not the boy they watched.

It was the idea.

He sat still in the velvet chair, heart cracking against his ribs, and realized he had become less a child than a chalice.

A vessel in red.

A glass box waiting for dust to gather inside.

When the prayers ended, the priest lifted a book from the lectern. Its cover was worn, corners blunted from too many hands. The way he held it suggested scripture, but Asael soon understood it was not the Word of God that was about to be spoken.

The priest cleared his throat. "These are the words of the faithful," he said.

And he began to read.

A woman's voice emerged through his mouth: "*When my child could not wake from fever, I placed a feather from the boy's steps beneath his pillow. By dawn, he breathed evenly. His cheeks were red with life.*"

Another: "*My husband's nightmares ceased the day he passed the boy on the road. He said a shadow lifted from him, a weight he had carried since war. He has not screamed in his sleep since.*"

And another, tremulous: "*I saw a light on the boy's hands as he lifted them in prayer. I thought I was seeing things. But when I looked again, the light was still there. I will never forget it.*"

Each voice was a confession, but not of sin, no. Each was a binding, a stitching of Asael into their wounds and their wonders.

He wanted to protest, to cry out, *It was not me!* He had never lifted a fever, never quelled a man's screaming nights. He had never set light on his hands. He had barely been here a day!

But the priest read on, steady and sure. The words were thick as incense. They pressed against Asael's ribs, weighed down his lungs.

The congregation whispered "Amen" after each testimony. Some wept openly, clasping hands until knuckles blanched. Others leaned forward, as though hungry for more, desperate to collect scraps of miracle with their ears.

And in the circle of candles, Asael sat motionless, his body stilled by the velvet's hold. His tongue pressed hard against the roof of his mouth, as though to keep it from betraying him.

He could feel it there, language, restless and dangerous. It stirred against the feathers still lodged deep in his throat, itching to break free. But he clamped down, swallowing until his eyes watered.

If I speak now, he thought, *what would they lose?*

The priest closed the book at last, the followed silence buzzing with devotion. Asael could feel it prickling his skin like static.

A robe was brought forth, folded neatly. White cord lay atop it. The villagers murmured their approval, and someone whispered "sacred."

The cloth was soft against his shoulders, but it did not warm him. It clung as if it were a binding, a garment for saints and captives alike.

Yet he wore it in silence.

And they praised him for it.

Even though the robe chafed at his neck.

Even though the white cord cinched across his chest like a leash.

And when he tried to shift in the velvet chair, it gave no relief—only reminded him of its grip.

The priest dismissed the congregation at last. Feet scuffed against stone, voices dipped low as people lingered to watch him rise. Some bowed. Others crossed themselves. A few simply stared in awe, lips parted as if expecting him to break open into light.

He did not. He only stood, the robe's hem dragging too heavy across the ground for a body in the form of a child.

When he stepped outside, the evening air was sharp, filled with the smoke of extinguished candles. The valley lay in a hush, as though waiting.

That was when he noticed them: the birds.

They clung to the windowsills, the chapel roof, the skeletal trees lining the yard. Black-feathered, grey-winged, some small as sparrows, others broad as hawks. None sang. Their silence was total, unnerving in its discipline.

Asael froze. For a heartbeat he thought they would descend on him, peck at his eyes, strip him bare. Maybe in some way, he wished they had. But they only watched, still as carvings. When he moved, a few lowered their heads, as if kneeling.

The villagers whispered. Some pointed, murmuring "signs," "confirmation," "blessing." Others pressed hands together and bent their knees on the dirt, mirroring the birds.

Asael turned away from their faces, from the silent vigil above. He hurried back to his cell, robe still binding him like a shroud.

Inside, he lit no candle. The dusk pooled in corners, deepening with each breath. His heart beat ragged.

He looked into the small silver chalice again.

The boy in its surface was not him.

Or rather, it was him, but staged. His own eyes returned his gaze, pale as washed linen, but they seemed emptied, hollowed, filled with something not his own. The robe gleamed brighter in reflection than in reality, as though the glass believed it holy even if he did not.

He raised his hand to the metal. His fingers touched the surface, but there was no answering weight, no sensation of skin meeting skin.

It was like pressing against water.

Like testing the edge of a dream.

The birds outside stirred, claws scraping against stone. He heard one wingbeat, heavy, then silence again.

He pulled his hand away, trembling. His breath fogged against the mirror. For an instant, it looked as though the reflection smiled without him.

The boy staggered back, heart hammering. His throat burned with words he dared not release, syllables clawing upward, begging to be known.

But he clenched his jaw. He would not give them sound.

Not while the glass was watching.

The fire claimed the house at the valley's edge. By dawn, the smoke had thinned, but its smell lingered—charred wood, wet ash, the acrid bite of grief that clung to hair and skin.

A child had been lost inside. The villagers gathered, their faces streaked with soot and tears. Some carried offerings of bread or herbs, others nothing but their silence.

The priest summoned Asael.

"You must speak," he said. "It will comfort them."

Asael shook his head, clutching at the robe's cord, but the priest placed a hand against his shoulder. The touch was light, almost tender, but there was no room for refusal.

The congregation parted as Asael stepped forward. The child's body lay shrouded in linen, small and still. Candles sputtered in the smoke-thick air, each flame trembling but refusing to die.

He stood at the front, and all eyes turned to him.

His legs shook under the robe, and the world felt as though it was shifting under him. The feathers in his throat quivered, begging to spread their blasphemy, yearning to take once more.

Yet, when he opened his mouth, his vision blurred.

His body chilled.

And the words came unbidden.

He could not recall choosing them, could not recall shaping them with tongue or teeth. They flowed like water through cracked stone, slow and unstoppable.

When he finished, silence fell.

Then the wailing began. Not the wailing of one, but of many. Mothers pressed their faces into children's hair, fathers clutched their sons close, strangers wept into strangers' arms.

Some called it a miracle. Others whispered proof.

Asael swayed on his feet, dizzy. He remembered nothing of what he had said, only the press of sound against his lips, the strange hollow afterward, as though he had poured himself out entirely.

But unlike before—unlike the sob in the convent or the whispers in the woods—nothing was taken from them. No memory dissolved. No faces vanished.

The words had been remembered.

The priest clasped Asael's hand as if sealing a covenant. "God speaks through you," he said, voice breaking with awe.

But Asael only felt emptied.

When night came, he lay awake, robe still clinging like damp skin. He thought of the child's shrouded body, of the villagers' tears, of the strange relief in their faces as though he had given them something they could not hold alone.

His chest ached with shame. He had wanted silence, but the world insisted on his voice. And now they treated it as holy.

The birds gathered again.

They lined his windowsill, unmoving. Even when he clapped his hands, even when he threw crumbs onto the sill, they remained. Their small black eyes glistened in the dark.

One, larger than the rest, fixed its gaze on him and did not blink all night.

Asael turned his face to the wall, but the weight of its watching pressed against him until dawn.

The first bird never moved.

Through the long stretch of the night, its eyes gleamed wet and still against the pane, refusing to cloud or close. Even when Asael turned from it, even when he pulled the blanket over his head, he felt its gaze. It threaded into his chest like a needle, stitching him to the silence of the room.

By dawn, others had come.

The sill was crowded—sparrows, starlings, a dove with a ragged wing. They pressed close as if summoned, feathers brushing glass, beaks tapping faintly now and then. Their weight made the frame groan.

The villagers whispered when they saw. "A sign," they said, voices hushed with awe. "The holy boy draws the living creatures."

Some knelt below the window. Others scattered seeds on the ground, as though feeding the birds meant feeding him. Someone lit a candle and placed it in the dirt. Its smoke curled upward and merged with the beating wings.

Asael stayed in bed, his throat raw, his tongue dry. The robe still clung to his shoulders from the day before, though he had not tied the cord. He could not shake the feeling that he was being wrapped in glass, sealed into something he had not chosen.

The birds did not sing. They only watched.

And the longer they watched, the thinner he felt.

When he finally dared to look in the mirror propped against the opposite wall, his reflection blinked a second too late. The glass did not quite match his movement—his hand raised, but the boy in the reflection hesitated, then followed. It was as though he were rehearsing himself, a shadow learning to keep up.

The priest entered at midday, smiling wide at the sight of the crowded sill. "Blessed one," he said. "Do you see? Even the creatures of the air testify to your holiness."

Asael lowered his eyes. He did not say that he only saw confinement. Not miracle. Not holiness. Surveillance.

When the priest left, he tried clapping again. The sound cracked in the small room, sharp and desperate. Still the birds remained. Only the dove blinked, once, slow as a closing door.

And that night, the vigil began anew.

He lay awake, the air thick with the smell of feathers and his skin prickling as though under endless hands. Every breath felt witnessed. Every turn in bed felt traced.

At some hour he could not name, he whispered—not words or syllables. Just a raw sound, low and broken. The birds did not scatter. Instead, their wings quivered as one, a tremor through the crowd.

Asael pressed his palm over his mouth.

He dreamed of glass that night. Glass caskets, glass jars, glass panes pressing him flat until he was no more than an image behind a transparent wall.

He woke with the taste of feathers in his throat.

XIV

It began with a scrap of cloth.

Someone swore it had come to them in a dream. A square of linen, faintly tinted with the shape of a boy's face. No brushstrokes, no needlework, only the impression of features pressed into fabric by sleep. When they brought it to the chapel, holding it aloft as though unveiling a relic, the sisters gathered and stared. The vague lines of eyes, mouth, hair. The faint shadow of wings above his shoulders.

"It is him," they whispered. "The boy."

Asael said nothing. He stood at the back, robe slipping from one shoulder, watching his likeness pass from hand to hand. The fabric did not look like him—it looked like something dreamed, softer, blurred at the edges, a face stripped of grief or hunger. He might have denied it, might have spoken, but the weight in his throat kept him still.

The cloth was laid before the altar, and candles burned around it. Pilgrims bent low, pressing lips to the fabric, murmuring prayers as though the thread itself could bless them. Someone wept into the linen until it darkened, then claimed the wet patch as proof of intercession.

This was where it started.

Within days, another image appeared. A painting on a thin plank of wood of a boy haloed in gold leaf, his lips closed in perfect silence. The painter swore their hand had been guided by God, that each stroke revealed what was already hidden within the wood. They titled it *The Boy in the Wall*.

The name lingered.

Soon after, a villager claimed that during matins she had seen an image forming on the plaster wall near the nave. A faint outline of a boy's face, pale and unfinished, as though pressed by breath through limewash. Another said the face had appeared in a scrap of linen left on the altar overnight, its faint weave holding the suggestion of hollow eyes and parted lips. No one admitted to painting, stitching, or carving anything. No one claimed ownership. The likeness was called a vision.

And so, he began to hear it in whispers.

At the well.

On the steps.

From the mouths of pilgrims who had never seen his face, yet pressed coins into the chapel's hands to glimpse the painted one.

Soon, the chapel was full of small tokens. A woman embroidered a handkerchief with feathers along the hem. A boy carved a wooden charm that showed a face with wings where its mouth should be. These were placed not at Asael's side, but in front of him—as though they could stand for him, replace him. He watched the objects accumulate, each a little less him, each a little more adored.

The whispers grew into certainty. Miracles followed these objects. An infant who would not quiet stilled when the embroidered handkerchief was laid on her chest. A widow swore that kissing the carved charm had lifted the weight from her lungs. Each testimony deepened Asael's unease. The more they praised the images, the less they looked at him.

The priest, encouraged, suggested a reliquary. A modest box, velvet-lined, to protect the cloth and plank. "Objects of holy witness," he said, nodding toward Asael as though the boy himself had approved.

The idea did not remain a suggestion for long.

On a grey morning thick with mist, the chapel bells rang not for lauds, but for what the priest called dedication. Villagers poured in, shawls damp from rain, children hushed by the occasion. The painted icon had been fitted with a thin gilt frame; the linen folded into a carved box of walnut lined with velvet.

Asael was placed near the altar. Not at its centre, not yet, but close enough that all eyes fell first on him, then on the objects meant to represent him.

The priest's voice carried through the nave, sonorous and certain: "These are not mere artifacts. They are signs. Proofs that God still walks among us. Proofs that He has chosen to speak through a vessel."

The word struck Asael like a stone. *Vessel.*

A divine word for the empty.

The reliquary was lifted, kissed, circled through the pews. Pilgrims pressed coins into the priest's hand as their lips touched the box, though he never asked for payment. A girl placed a sprig of lavender inside, "so the holy boy's sleep would be sweet." An old man swore his back pain eased when his fingers brushed the wood. Every gesture, every murmur, wrapped Asael tighter in the glass cage he felt forming.

He tried to step back, but someone steadied him—thinking he faltered not from dread, but awe.

"Be proud," they whispered. "This honour is yours."

Honor. He looked at the cloth, blurred and false. At the plank, its painted lips sealed. They looked more like him to the crowd than he did standing there alive, in flesh and silence.

The priest raised his arms, declaring: "From this day, the Boy in the Wall is not merely among us, but beyond us. He belongs to heaven, and heaven has lent him to us awhile."

The villagers knelt. A sea of bent heads, shoulders trembling with tears.

Asael did not kneel.

His reflection caught in the reliquary's polished lock. The face that stared back was not his—too calm, too gilded, too contained. He wondered if this was the moment he had been buried alive. Not in earth, but in belief.

He tried to breathe, but even air felt like glass sliding down his throat.

Asael's reflection appeared in unexpected places after that. In the polish of the brass candlesticks, in the sheen of holy water, in the fragments of glass fitted into the chapel windows. He would catch sight of himself and feel a slippage—as though he were watching someone else wear his face, a silent actor whose gestures never matched the thoughts inside his chest.

It unsettled him more than the silence of his throat.

He overheard them speak of him when they thought him out of earshot. They did not call him Asael. They did not ask what he hungered for, or if his nights were cold. They said "hope," "penance," "miracle." They said, "He is not of this world."

He wanted to ask them what world they thought he belonged

to, if not this one.

But the words stayed trapped, sharp as glass, in his lungs.

A child was brought to him one morning, cradled by a mother whose eyes were red with exhaustion. The infant cried ceaselessly, wailing with a force that shook its small ribs. The woman placed the child at Asael's feet and begged.

He did not know what she wanted.

But something in him moved—an instinct, a memory of lullabies Sister Elene had hummed once long ago. He let the tune slip through his lips, fragile, low. Not words, only melody.

The infant stilled. Its breathing slowed. The chapel filled with the stunned silence of a miracle.

Afterward, they whispered that the boy's voice soothed even babes. That he could silence storms. That his breath itself was sanctified.

The cloth grew heavier with kisses. The plank glowed with fresh gilding.

And Asael felt thinner each day.

Not of this world, they said. Not flesh, not blood.

But he was. He bled when he tore feathers from his throat. He starved when food was withheld. He shivered when wind struck through the cracks of his chamber.

Still, when he looked in the brass, he did not recognize himself. The boy staring back wore the face of an icon. Not hungry, not wounded, not ashamed. A mask of sanctity painted smooth over the hollows of his body.

The Boy in the Wall.

He wondered which one would remain when the other disappeared.[13]

---

13   *"The physician came by again to draw more blood. I hate getting blood drawn. Perhaps they'll use it to clone me."*

XV

Hell had opened, and it began with a feather.

Not one Asael shed with grace, not one folded neatly into the pages of his manuscript, but one that fell from him as he slept. It drifted onto the stone floor outside the crude cot they had given him, soft, pale, and smaller than most.

At dawn, a pilgrim bent to lift it. The woman pressed it between her palms as though it were the host, tears running down her cheeks. She whispered a name Asael did not recognize—perhaps a sick son, perhaps a long-dead husband—and when she left, she carried the feather hidden in her bodice, clutching it as though she had stolen God Himself.

The next morning, another feather was gone. A novice had plucked it from his bedding, tucking it into the lining of her stole. She kissed the spot where she had slipped it, whispering prayers of gratitude as though she had earned some divine appointment. Asael noticed the faint sting in his shoulder where it had been torn free. The ache lingered longer than any ordinary wound.

Then, a ragged plume that tore loose as he turned in his sleep. It lay broken on the stone, its quill still glistening with the thin red bead where it had ripped from his skin.

At dawn, a pilgrim bent to lift it. The woman pressed it between her palms and kissed it, muttering prayers and praise. She did not see the blood still wet at its base. Or perhaps she did, and that made it holier.

The next day, a novice slipped a downy tuft into the lining of her stole, smiling as though the tiny filament alone might save her soul. Asael noticed the bald, weeping patch it left behind. It stung when touched, and the flesh there felt softer, thinner—like skin peeled once too often.

By the week's end, pilgrims had begun to crowd closer to him, watching for when the smallest plume shook loose. Their eyes glistened with feverish hunger. They vied to be the first to reach the floor, to snatch the fallen token as if it were manna.

Soon, his body became their harvest.

They came closer, each day braver and bolder, until fingers brushed his shoulders without permission, tugging loose what had not yet fallen. Each pluck was not a neat theft but a tearing of flesh drawn upward, pores stretched wide, tiny veins bursting. The sound was soft but unbearable—like parchment ripping near the ear.

Blood dotted his collar, his sleeves, the sheets where he slept. Pilgrims gathered the stained fabric as fervently as the feathers themselves. Some pressed the broken shafts into wounds, believing the sting would heal them. One mother held a quill to her infant's gums until it wailed blood. She smiled through her own tears. "He will never know sickness again."

When Asael's feathers grew back, they came in crooked, thin, fragile. But those too were plucked before they could root deep, leaving his body patchy, ragged, raw. His shoulders shivered with phantom wings—empty sockets opening where once there had been fullness.

Candles wept constantly before the reliquary, but near Asael they bled strange. Thick gouts of wax slid down their sides like melting skin, congealing in lumps that hardened into crude forms—winged shapes, crying mouths, faces caught in mid-scream.

The villagers called it miracle wax. They broke off shards and swallowed them. Some melted the grotesque lumps down to pour into the molds of crosses, beads, charms. Asael once saw a man press a hardened lump against his tongue, shudder, and whisper, "Sweet."

But the wax was not sweet. He had smelled it while they scraped it from the stones near his cot—rank, acrid, almost like scorched fat. When he touched it by accident, the oil clung to his skin and would not wash off.

One night Asael woke to find Sister Alene kneeling at the foot of his cot, scraping the stone beneath his bedding for hardened remnants of candle wax that had dripped too far. "Forgive me, child." She whispered with fervour. "It is only for their healing."

By then, men from neighbouring villages had begun arriving at the chapel, bearing gifts. Bolts of raw silk. Clay jars of salt. Dried fish. They did not lay these before the altar as offerings to God. They pressed them into the steward's hands, begging in return for blessings—words, touches, relics of holiness from Asael himself.

The steward's face gleamed with possibility. He saw not only faith but currency. He whispered to the priest of markets, of pilgrimage, of how relics might be carefully catalogued, blessed, and distributed for a tithe.

And so, the trade began.

Men began arriving with silk, salt, jars of honey. They pushed gifts at the steward in exchange for blessings, and the steward—eyes glittering—made his plans.

Thus, Asael's chamber had become a stall.

Pilgrims were ushered in pairs, and when they knelt, they did so not in prayer but with a deepening hunger. The steward guided their hands.

"Take gently," he said. "He is fragile."

But the hands were never gentle. They dug into Asael's skin,

153

pinching, tugging until something tore free. Sometimes the feather came away clean, leaving behind a raw dot of blood. Other times the quill snapped under the nail, jagged, splintered, still rooted deep. Those pieces festered. His shoulders burned, sores opening, sticky with pus that pilgrims wiped on their veils as if holy oil.

A man once knelt and sank his teeth into the root of a feather at Asael's wrist. The scream that tore from Asael's throat was soundless—he had taught himself not to make sound—but his body shook as blood poured down his hand. The man wept as he swallowed the shaft whole. "Praise be, Amen."

The pain was not like ordinary injury. Each feather plucked left not only blood but some form of absence. A hollowing. As though what had been taken carried part of him with it—breath, memory, warmth. He grew paler, slower. His chest sank inward. He felt his heart beat against the cage of ribs more sharply, as though there was less of him left to muffle its sound.

When he looked in the mirror polished brass of the reliquary latch, he barely recognized the creature staring back. His face seemed thinner, his eyes wider and sunken, his lips cracked and mouth more like a wound with ragged feathers. He wondered if soon there would be nothing left of him but feathers and wax. Something not human. Not angel. Something in between, used until emptied.

At night, he dreamt of the plucking continuing long after his body gave out. Strangers bending over him, tearing feather after feather until only bones remained, and even those taken, ground, swallowed, preserved. he dreamt of his body splitting apart like a plucked fowl, skin peeled back, quills yanked in clumps until nothing was left but a cage of bone and the soft sound of tearing. He sometimes woke with the sensation that entire ribs were missing, only to find them still there, fragile but intact.

He woke once to find three pilgrims around his cot. They

had cut his nightshirt away, stripping feathers from his chest as though harvesting grain.

Their hands were wet.

He vomited onto the floor.

"I'm scared..."

One of them whispered, "A gift."

One evening, an elder sister finally spoke. She rose during supper, voice trembling.

"This cannot be reverence." The words were barely a whisper, but she held true. "This is desecration. You strip the boy as if he were an altar cloth. You consume him piece by piece and call it holy. You eat the boy alive. You grind his body into charms and call it devotion."

The hall fell silent. Then the steward rose, hands spread, voice firm:

"Sister, it is precisely reverence. Preservation is proof. Faith demands relics. Would you deny the people the grace they find in him? Would you deny them healing? Every feather is a blessing. Every drop of blood a promise. Would you shame the Lord's work?"

Others nodded. "It is love," they murmured. "It is devotion." "It is reverence." It is how saints are remembered."

The elder sister's eyes met Asael's across the room. Her lips shaped words he could not hear—perhaps *forgive me*. But she sat down, and no more protests followed.

And so the hunger grew.

From then on, he was never left whole. Every hour another hand reached. Every day another quill torn free. He could feel the emptiness gathering inside, as though his marrow were being sucked away feather by feather. His chest was all hollows, his breath shallow, each exhale rattling like an emptied cage.

155

Pilgrims pressed their lips to his wounds, smearing blood across their mouths as though consuming the Eucharist itself.

He was not preserved.

He was consumed.

He could no longer walk the chapel without someone reaching for him, brushing his sleeve, searching for a loose feather to claim. When he slept, he dreamt of hands plucking him bald, of skin peeling back to reveal endless rows of feathers packed beneath, each tug a theft of self until nothing was left but a trembling husk, hollow as an eggshell.

He pressed his hands against his chest, trying to hold himself together, but the hollow remained.

The reliquary glowed brighter each day. The candles wept faster. The villagers whispered louder.

And Asael, feather by feather, drop by drop, was forced to be unmade.

XVI

The chapel bells rang, not for liturgy. Asael had thought it was for mourning, but quickly learned it was celebration. Villagers came carrying bread and dried fruit, honey in clay pots, garlands of early spring blossoms. The nave was draped with ribbons, altar cloths replaced with fresh linen. Asael was led forward, not asked, not guided, but positioned.

A dais had been built from wooden planks. Upon it was placed a chair higher than any he had sat in before. They pressed him into it. A crown of woven vines settled on his head, damp with dew. Garlands looped over his shoulders, flowers tangling with the broken shafts of feathers that still clung to his skin.

The steward raised his hands, and his voice boomed.

"Today we give thanks for the boy who walks among us. Today we speak his name, that heaven itself may hear it and be glad."

The crowd responded as one. Their voices rose, chanting:

"Asael! Asael! Asael!"

He had not told them his name.

At first it felt only strange. But as the sound repeated, as the syllables rolled through the nave in unison, he felt his chest tighten.

His name had once been a private thing, whispered by Sister Elene with tenderness. A gift. A prayer. Now it was no longer his. Each time they said it, it slipped further from him, becoming an offering he never asked to receive. One that broke everything within him. The name made him now sick.

A child touched his wrist, small fingers curling around the place where feathers had been torn. The boy whispered, "Thank you for still being here."

The words pierced deeper than any plucking. Still being here. As though his life, his body, were not his own, but property maintained for their sake.

The chant rose louder. *Asael!*

Asael!

ASAEL!

He caught glimpses of himself in polished brass plates, in the wet sheen of tears on faces, in the curve of a spoon left glinting on the altar. His reflection fractured, multiplied. Each face looked less like him, more like the painted boy in the reliquary, the icon stitched into cloth. Smaller, thinner, until he was hardly present at all.

The chant filled the rafters, pressed against his ribs, made his pulse stumble. He felt himself dissolving under the sound, syllable by syllable.

Something in him trembled. The urge to answer surged up—one word, any word, to reclaim his name. His lips parted. He felt the feathers shift in his throat, the sharp edge of voice pressing forward.

But he knew the cost. A word spoken would not come free. It would pull memory from someone in the crowd; a father's laughter, a daughter's prayer, a widow's last image of her husband's face.

He could give them his voice, but only by stealing something in return. And even in his suffering and misery, he did not want to curse them.

His mouth closed. His throat burned.

The chanting went on.

ASAEL! ASAEL! ASAEL![14]

When night fell and the revellers staggered home, leaving petals strewn across the nave, Asael slipped away. The dais loomed behind him, crowned with abandoned garlands already wilting.

He passed a bowl of water left on a bench. His reflection stared back at him in the ripples—gaunt, crowned with vines, mouth bloodied at the corners. He did not recognize the boy in the water.

They called it a blessing.

But Asael could not help but wonder what had been lost to make space for it.

---

14   *"They keep chanting. They won't... I can't..."*

CASSETTE 006

[Click.]

[A faint hiss, followed by a long pause. Then a shallow inhale. His voice is very soft, as if he's unsure anyone should hear this.]

There's a room in the chapel that's always locked.

Glass cabinets. Old books. Bones in velvet-lined boxes.

They call it the reliquary. The room for things too precious to touch.

Today, they unlocked it.

They let me walk through. Not to look—but to show someone else through. And when I stepped inside, Sister Eliane said, "Careful, Errevale. You belong in here."

She meant it kindly. I smiled like it was kind.

But something in me went still.

[He shifts, barely. A creak of wood.]

I know what she meant.

That I'm important. Special.

That people will want to remember me.

But all I could think was 'You don't bury living boys in glass.'

[Another pause. His voice gets even quieter.]

I don't think they see me anymore.

I think they see what they want me to be.

Something soft and brilliant and not quite real.

They whisper about me like I'm not in the room.

They ask if I've had new visions,

if I've written anything holy,

if I've felt "closer to the voice."

No one asks if I'm okay.

The birds still come to my windows.

I counted seven this morning.

They don't sing. They just watch.

Maybe that's what I'm for now.
To be watched.

Not spoken to.
Not touched.
Not held.

Just… observed.
Like an icon. Or a warning, maybe.
Like a body that stopped being a person.

[The sound of fabric moving, as if he's wrapped in a blanket. A little static.]

I used to think being loved meant being safe.
But now it feels like being trapped.

Like I'm being wrapped in something sacred. So no one has to touch the messy parts.

They say they love me., bbut they never ask what I want.

Or what I need.

Or who I miss.

I suppose because saints don't need things.

And relics don't mourn.

[He exhales, slow and even. A soft creak—maybe his bed, maybe the recorder shifting.]

I remember when I was held without trembling.

Before the stories. Before the books.

Someone held my hand after I fell on the steps.

They didn't say anything holy.

They didn't call me chosen.

They just… helped me up.

I don't think anyone's touched me since.

Not like that.

Not without…

[A faint breeze passes the mic. He speaks again, even softer.]

I think I'm being kept in a glass box.

And the worst part is… They don't think it's a box at all.
They think it's a gift.
But I…
I'm…

[A long silence.]

Goodnight.

[Click.]

IV

CASSETTE 007

[Click.]

[A wet static hum. A long silence. Then a sharp inhale.]

They used to bow their heads when I walked by. But now they hold their breath.

It feels heavier than silence. Like waiting for thunder. Like something in me has become the storm they expect.

[He exhales slowly. The sound of his thumb rubbing against the recorder's mic, restless.]

No one told me what my body would do. Not the priests. Not the sisters. They preached purity, chastity, abstinence. They warned of "animal hungers" and sins that rot the soul. But never once did they tell me what it means to wake up shaking, drenched, my own skin betraying me.

[He pauses, taking a shaky breath.]

I find myself staring too long at them. At the curve of a throat, or the shape of a hand resting on a hymn book. The line of a shoulder where robe meets skin. And then I feel sick— like I've swallowed glass. Because I was taught that this was filth. That desire is a wound you give yourself. But it's in me anyway, coiled hot in my belly, crawling beneath my skin like something hatched.

[He shifts. Fabric rustles as though he's drawn his knees up.]

They look at me differently now. Not just with reverence. With... hunger.

I see it in the novices' eyes when I pass. I see it in the way an older brother held his breath as I bent to lift a dropped chalice, the way his gaze clung to the back of my neck, the way he crossed himself after—as if to hide the staring inside the prayer.

And I hate it. Sainthood is pure. Sainthood in without sin. Yet I find myself... wanting. Wanting the gaze. Even as it strips me into pieces, turns me into nothing but what they want.

[He pauses. His voice lowers, fevered, ashamed.]

My hands burn now. Not just warm, but alive. When someone brushes past me, I feel the memory of it for hours. Sometimes I wake with my own fists clenched tight around the sheets, sticky with... something I don't understand. It feels wrong. Unholy. Yet when I press my palms together to pray, the tremor doesn't stop. It only worsens.

[He sighs deeply.]

I caught my reflection today. My jaw is sharper. My chest broader. My voice sounds different when I speak aloud. It's lower, stranger, like someone else has grown inside my ribs. I don't recognize the face. I don't recognize the body. But they do. They look at me like it's proof of something. Like the change itself is divine.

[He laughs once, harsh and short—It breaks into a breathless sound closer to fear than humour.]

I hate that I wrote that book. I hate that they took the ramblings of a child and turned them into divinity. Perhaps if I had burned it...

I... I don't want to be holy. I don't want to be a vessel for their prayers, their hunger, their secret shames whispered into the walls. But this body—my body— isn't mine anymore. It's theirs. An altar they kneel to. A temptation they whisper about. A relic they'd touch if they dared.

And me? I don't know if I'm revolted or... or curious. I don't know which is worse.

[His voice trembles, softer now, each word exhaled as if it costs something.]

God is distance. That's what I've come to believe. Not love. Not safety. Just distance. Because what's holy is never allowed to touch. Never allowed to be touched.

And yet... I ache to be touched. Even as it terrifies me. Even as I pray for it to go away.

[Silence. A faint sound like teeth against a thumbnail. Then, low;]

I think I'm becoming something I was never taught to name. And it feels like blasphemy just to admit it.

[He breathes in. A long pause. Then, so softly it is nearly swallowed by static;]

Goodnight.

[Click]

XVII

The fever began in silence.

Asael first noticed it when his skin no longer cooled with the evening air. The wind slipped between the trees like a silver blade, cold enough to shiver the leaves into their nighttime hymn, but his flesh did not shiver with them. He burned from within, a quiet fire that licked through marrow and into blood, making every heartbeat a molten pulse.

He pressed his palm to his chest, felt the tremor of his ribs. They seemed too hot to belong to him. Too alive.

By dawn, his skin gleamed with sweat. Droplets beaded at his temples, along his collarbone, soaking the linen at his throat. When he moved, his garments clung like wet bandages.

The villagers called it a sign.

They came with bowls of blessed ice water, pressing damp cloths to his wrists and brow, whispering as though their words might coax the fever into prophecy. Their hands were careful, trembling less so from pity and more from reverence, as if touching his burning flesh was akin to touching the chalice or the host. Some caught his sweat on their fingertips and brought it reverently to their lips.

One woman dabbed the damp from his neck with a scrap of cloth. She tucked the square into her sleeve as though she had stolen a relic, and her eyes shone with the fever of belief.

They did not speak to him. They spoke about him. They spoke around him. Blessed heat, they called it. A sacred fire. Proof of the angel trapped in flesh.

Asael tried to tell them it was sickness, that his lungs burned, that his muscles trembled as though hollowed by hunger. But when his lips parted, no words came. Only breath, thick and steaming, that left their eyes shining brighter.

He dreamed of feathers.

They pushed from places they did not belong. His hips, his thighs, the tender webbing between his fingers. Each quill broke the skin like a needle forced through cloth, parting flesh in slow, deliberate shreds. Blood welled around their shafts, hot as the fever burning him from within, and trickled down his body in thin rivulets that pooled at his ankles.

In the dream, he tried to pull them out. His nails hooked beneath their barbs, tearing skin as he wrenched the pale shafts free. Each feather slid from his body with a soft tearing sound, wet and fibrous, as if pulled from the roots of his veins. The wounds they left gaped like mouths, and the air hissed through them with every ragged breath.

When he looked down, the feathers covered him—thighs matted with blood and down, hands trembling, chest quivering with quills that forced themselves up from beneath his sternum. His palms split open as feathers pressed outward, curling into the air like skeletal fingers.

The villagers were in the dream, too. They knelt before him, eyes wide with worship. One reached forward to pluck a dripping feather from his thigh. Another held out a chalice to catch the blood falling from his hand. They whispered holy, holy, holy as his body ruptured into plumage.

"Errevale! It is time to bathe."
He woke choking on his own breath, linen plastered to his skin. His chest heaved. His palms stung.
"Ah... of course Sister. Coming..."

In the light of dawn, his sheets were scattered with down.

Not dream-feathers. Real ones. White as bone, damp with the sheen of sweat.

He pressed them into a bundle, hid them beneath his bedding, and tried not to look at the red indentations where they had torn through the skin of his hands.

But when he closed his eyes, he still felt them growing.

By the second night, Asael could barely stand. His body shook with each step, with bones hollow as reeds and every breath dragging fire through his chest. He tried to drink from the stream, but the water tasted of ash. He tried to eat, but his mouth filled with feathers instead of bread.

When he stumbled, they caught him. Gentle, reverent hands—not lifting him as one might a sick boy, but as if bearing an offering from one altar to another.

They laid him down in the chapel's nave. Candles burned on either side, their flames guttering as if they too strained to breathe. Sisters pressed cool cloths to his skin, changing them often, carrying the soaked linens away as if they were relics too holy to discard. Some cut the damp squares into pieces to be folded into prayer-books. Others pressed them to their lips.

One knelt close enough that he felt her breath against his face. "The angel's fire burns for us," she whispered.

Asael wanted to scream. To tell them that he was afraid of the heat inside him, of the feathers blooming in his flesh, of the blood that came too easily when he touched his own skin.

But still nothing came. Only a ragged exhale that smelled of iron and smoke.

The villagers bowed their heads as if the breath itself were benediction. They gathered close, whispering thanks, brushing their fingers over his wrists, his damp hair, the edge of his trembling mouth.

He shut his eyes. His body was no longer his own.

That night, he dreamed of himself laid in a reliquary of glass, his skin slick with sweat, his feathers pressed flat against the walls. People passed by, gazing at him with eyes like empty chalices, waiting for him to fill them.

And he woke with the taste of ashes on his tongue.

XVIII

The first time the fire came, it did not announce itself.

It woke him.

Asael's body was drenched, his skin slick as if he had been pulled from a basin of boiling water. His sheets clung to him in clammy folds. The feathers at the back of his neck itched and hissed against the pillow, their barbs faintly smouldering as though something had brushed them with coal. He bolted upright with a gasp, clutching at his chest, certain that something outside had caught fire—that the chapel roof had fallen into flames or that the forest had lit with lightning.

But there was no smoke in the air, no crackling beyond the walls.

The fire was inside him.

His throat tasted of iron and ash. When he exhaled, the damp air seemed to waver as if he were breathing out heat. He pressed his palms against his skin, dragging them from chest to belly to thighs, and found every inch of him burning, fever-lit. His blood raced as though it had been replaced with molten wax. His mouth hung open, but no sound escaped—only the rasp of breath drawn too fast, too shallow.

He tried to pray, his mouth moving in soundless words of revelry.

But the words stuck, blistering at the edge of his tongue.

He flung the sheets aside, crawling onto the stone floor in search of coolness. The flagstones felt icy at first, but within moments they warmed beneath him, sweat seeping from his body as though it sought escape. He dragged his cheek along the stone, smearing salt and damp, mouthing syllables that broke into panting gasps.

When he slept again, it was a fever-sleep, thick with dreams of smoke filling his lungs, of wings beating within his ribs, their feathers singed black and fragile, crumbling when he tried to touch them.

The next morning, a family came to the chapel with offerings. Bread wrapped in a cloth, a vial of salt, three silver buttons from a soldier's uniform. They were poor, their clothes ragged, but they bowed with the reverence of pilgrims who had travelled days. The mother's eyes were wide, wet with awe; the father held his son by the shoulders, guiding him forward as if presenting him for blessing.

Asael sat on the bench where they had placed him, still shivering from the night. His robe clung damp to his body. He tried to make himself small, folding his hands, lowering his head so his hair shadowed his face.

But when the family drew near, the fever stirred.

Heat surged from his chest outward, crawling up his throat, spilling into his cheeks. The air around him shimmered faintly. His breathing quickened, chest rising too fast. Sweat trickled from his hairline, dripping onto the collar of his robe.

The mother gasped. She fell to her knees.

"Blessed child," she whispered. "The fire of the Lord is in him."

Her son knelt, trembling. The father bowed so low his forehead struck the stone.

Asael pressed his lips together, tasting blood where his

teeth cut his tongue. He could feel his body betraying him, this unwanted heat blazing brighter in their nearness. The closer they came, the more the fire inside him strained to escape—as though they themselves fed it, their presence like kindling. He wanted to cry out, to tell them to leave, to stop looking at him.

But he said nothing.

He only burned.

That night, the fire worsened.

"God forgive me for I have sinned. I am impure..."

His hands would not still; they trembled against his ribs, against his thighs, against the place where his pulse beat so hot it frightened him. His skin flushed dark, blotched as if bruised by unseen hands. His feathers fell one by one, drifting into his lap, but when he lifted them, their edges were blackened, curled by heat.

He gagged and coughed, body convulsing, until feathers spilled from his mouth—slick and pale, their tips scorched. They littered the floor in a ring around him. His throat burned raw, the taste of smoke coating every swallow.

When he lifted his head, the chamber reeked of singed down.

The villagers found the feathers in the morning. They carried them into the nave, pressing them to their foreheads, whispering that they were blessed, that they would heal burns and fever.

No one asked how he had coughed them up.

No one asked if it hurt.

In his dream fled into the woods to cool himself.

He found a stream that coiled between moss-dark rocks and lowered himself into it, plunging his fevered body beneath the current. For a moment, the water soothed him, the chill numbing his skin. He pressed his face into the streambed, letting the current

181

choke and cleanse him.

But then the water hissed.

Where it touched his flesh, bubbles rose, steam lifting in curls. The moss nearest his hands browned, curling inward. The stream grew cloudy, feather-fragments breaking loose from his lips and throat, floating downstream like shed ash.

He staggered back, drenched, gasping. The water clung hot to his skin, his robe plastered to him like molten cloth. His body radiated warmth that refused to leave him.

And he thought, *I am unclean.*

Not holy. Not chosen.

I am sick.

A sickness given form in his blood, his voice, his feathers.

That night, he lay alone, shivering in his fever-heat. He did not dare pray aloud. He pressed his hands against his chest, whispering the only words he trusted: *stop, stop, stop!*

But the fire refused to be quelled.

It grew.

And when he finally drifted into sleep again, he dreamed of burning whole—his body split open, feathers crackling into cinders, his throat spilling flame instead of song. Villagers gathered around, kneeling, praising the light, weeping with joy as they warmed themselves in his ruin.

And Asael woke to the taste of ash, certain that his body had already begun to betray him.

XVIX

The fever did not relent. If anything, it sharpened into awareness—not of himself, but of the air between him and others. Every movement through the chapel was a negotiation with distance. He felt their breath on his skin before they drew near. He sensed the shift in silence when someone reached toward him. He could taste the salt of their anticipation on his tongue before fingers grazed him.

It began with accidents.

Or what he was told were accidents.

A woman kneeling at the altar let her hand slip from the pew, brushing the hem of his robe as he passed. She murmured an apology, though her eyes never lifted from his fabric. A novice setting down a basin of water allowed her knuckles to graze his ankle, then linger there longer than necessary. A pilgrim girl, clumsy and bright-eyed, pressed too close, his palm flat against Asael's thigh before being pulled away by a trembling mother.

None of them pulled back quickly.

Each touch was met with a pause, as if stealing bits and bits of him in their wake.

When they withdrew, Asael felt both relieved and hollow. His body shook faintly, as if his nerves could not decide whether to recoil or reach back. His throat tightened. The fever within him flared, answering touch with heat, answering closeness with trembling.

He told himself it was sickness.

But his body did not listen.

One morning, as he left the chapel, he felt fabric pressed against his neck. Startled, he turned and saw an old woman clutching the square of linen she had dabbed against his skin. His sweat gleamed on the cloth like oil. She folded it into her palm with reverence, as though she had been handed balm for the dying.

"Blessed," she whispered. "Blessed warmth."

Others saw.

Others followed.

Soon they came with cloths hidden in sleeves, brushing them against his skin when he least expected—his wrist, his temple, the small of his back. He flinched but never cried out, and each time they took what he shed as though it were sacrament. His sweat was bottled. His heat captured.

Asael began to dread his own body more than his voice.

His voice at least could be withheld.

But his body betrayed him without permission.

He overheard them in whispers.

"The angel is warm." "Warmth means blessing." "His heat is proof."

The words horrified him. They stripped his warmth of its shame, painting sickness as miracle. But Asael knew better. He had felt his flesh blister, his feathers burn black at the edges. He had watched the water hiss against his skin. If this was blessing than he had learned that blessing was rot.

Yet they worshipped it.

He could not stop them.

One evening, the steward summoned him.

The chamber smelled of wine and parchment, of melted wax cooling in long drips across the floor. Maps and ledgers lay spread across the table. The steward's eyes glistened with hunger Asael recognized, but not the hunger of prayer.

"Your presence," the steward said softly, "is bringing them. Pilgrims by the dozens. By the hundreds soon. They leave coins, cloth, rings, bread, anything for a glimpse. And they all ask for a touch. Do you see what this means?"

Asael stared at him in silence.

The steward leaned forward, voice low and fervent. "It means we must not waste this gift. We must prepare for the influx. Blessing is not only for the spirit—it feeds the body, the land, the chapel itself. God has given us a resource. We must harvest it wisely."

Harvest.

The word sank into Asael's chest and filled him with dread.

He imagined himself divided—pieces parcelled out like relics, skin flayed into ribbons, feathers sold like precious silk, sweat collected in vials as balm for the dying. His flesh displayed, his heat bartered, his body sold in fragments until nothing remained but an empty husk, glowing faintly with what they called holy.

He gripped the edge of the chair, his hands slick with his own fever.

The steward smiled as though speaking to a chalice. "They will come from kingdoms away. They will kneel. They will pay. The blessing is not yours to keep. It is ours to share."

Asael lowered his gaze to the stone floor, breath stuttering in his throat. He thought of the cloths pressed to his skin, the hands grazing his body, the linen folded around drops of his sweat. He thought of the whispers; *warmth means blessing.*

And for the first time, he wondered if he hated the heat inside his body more than the silence in his throat.

That night, alone in his cell, Asael pressed his palms to his chest and whispered into the fever; *Stop. Stop. Please, enough...*

But the fire only grew, pulsing hotter, hungrier, until his skin burned as though waiting for the next hand to steal from him.

He curled into himself, trembling, and understood at last that his body no longer belonged to him.

It had been claimed.

Turned into sacrament.

Desecrated by reverence.

And he was left inside it, trapped, burning, praying not for salvation but for stillness.[15]

---

15   *"God give me strength, the flesh is weak but you are strong."*

XX

It lived under his skin like a second heart, throbbing in waves of fire. Each time someone brushed near him, it leapt higher, scorching through his veins as though begging to be touched, consumed. The villagers saw holiness in it. Asael felt only invasion. He could no longer tell if the fire belonged to him or if he had truly become a vessel for something else entirely.

He decided, at last, that it had to be stopped.

If not by prayer or silence, then by force.

The first thing he tried was rope.

He stole a length from the chapel storeroom, meant for binding hay bales, and wound it tightly around his chest. He cinched it until the fibres dug into his skin, until the shallow rise and fall of his breathing felt like knives scraping his ribs. He thought perhaps if the chest could not swell, the fire would have no air to burn.

But it burned hotter.

The rope left deep welts across his torso, purple and red where the skin swelled around the cord. By morning, blood had seeped in thin lines from where the fibres had cut him. His feathers stuck to it, clotted in place, tearing free when he tried to unwind the rope.

The sight of his own blood sickened him.

And yet—he felt relief.

For a moment, the fire flinched.

The next night, he used a strip of linen. He threaded it with a sharpened quill and sewed the linen directly into his skin—small stitches across his chest, pulling the flesh taut to trap the heat beneath. His hands shook hard as he worked, blood bubbling around each puncture as his bones begged him to stop. The thread gleamed wet and dark in the candlelight.

He gasped with every stitch. Each hole burned, each tug sent a jolt of fire up his arms as he forced down sobs on pain.

But when it was done, he pressed his hand to the bound flesh and felt, just for a breath, silence.

The fire still roared within, but muffled, like a storm behind heavy shutters.

The third night, he turned to his mouth.

He could taste the salt of his sweat on others' cloths, hear their whispers about his warmth. His body had been stolen. He would not let his voice follow.

From the reliquary, he stole a needle meant for mending vestments. He held it over the flame of a candle until it glowed faintly red, then threaded it with golden silk left as offering by a pilgrim.

And in the quiet of his cell, he sewed his lips shut.

The first pierce tore a scream from him—but it stayed locked inside, muffled by the blood filling his mouth. His tongue convulsed against the needle, slicing itself open. Feathers, slick with red, slid up his throat and choked him until he gagged them onto the floor.

But stitch by stitch, he closed himself.

The golden silk gleamed with saliva and blood, taut across his mouth like a mockery of sanctity. Each tug forced his lips together until they split, swollen and cracked. His face throbbed with heat. Tears burned down his cheeks.

When it was finished, he lay trembling on the floor. His breath hissing through his nose, wet and ragged. The fire within him screamed to be released, but now it had no exit. It battered against the silk.

Blood leaked down his chin, pooling on the stone. Feathers stuck to it, matted in gore.

And Asael smiled through the pain, thinking, *At last. My body is mine.*

But the body betrays.

Within days, his stitches festered. The silk, once bright, grew black with rot. Pus wept from the holes, mingling with the blood until his chin crusted with filth. His skin split around the stitches, tearing the wounds wider. His throat filled with the taste of iron, copper, and ash.

Still, he did not unbind himself.

Instead, he cut deeper.

He pressed broken shards of glass against his thighs and arms, carving channels for the heat to bleed. He watched in dizzy fascination as the blood spilled, steaming faintly, carrying with it tiny fragments of feathers singed at the tips. His body coughed itself out onto the floor in pieces: down clumps, slicked with gore; ribbons of skin curling from his cuts; sweat dripping into the wounds and hissing like hot oil.

Every act of harm brought a kind of ecstasy—shame mingled with relief, as if for every shred he destroyed, a fragment of the villagers' grasp slipped away.

His cell became a shrine of blood. Feathers had plastered the walls, sticking to the stone with drying clots. The floor was slick, stained dark where he pressed his wounds to drain them. His bedding smelled of copper and salt, ruined beyond repair.

But still the fire burned.

It would not be killed.

One particular night, delirious with fever and pain, Asael staggered to the mirror the steward had hung in his chamber to impress pilgrims. Its brass surface reflected him dimly, warped at the edges, but he could see enough.

What stared back was no boy.

His face was swollen, silk threads pulling his mouth into a grotesque, blood-crusted smile. His chest was bound with rope and linen, welts glowing red where the flesh bulged against its bindings. His arms dripped with cuts, feathers tangled in the wounds like parasites.

The reflection did not blink.

It breathed, shallow and rattling, as though mocking his attempt at control.

Asael raised his trembling hand and pressed it to the glass. His palm left a smear of blood across the surface, obscuring the image.

For a moment, he imagined he could erase himself entirely.

But the reflection remained.

Alive. Burning. Desecrated.

And behind it, faintly—like a figure watching through the glass—something smiled.

XXI

When the sisters entered his cell at dawn, they froze in the doorway. Blood streaked the stone walls, feathers clotted in piles across the floor. Rope lay slack around his chest, soaked dark, while the linen stitches across his lips glistened with pus and fresh crimson.

One whispered a prayer. Another whispered "miracle."

They did not recoil.

They bowed.

Within hours, word spread. Pilgrims poured into the chapel, their faces pale, their eyes glistening. They crowded at the threshold, gasping at the sight of Asael bound and bleeding, his skin torn open in ribbons.

"Stigmata," someone breathed. "Proof."

Hands reached for his wounds. They pressed cloths to his chest, catching the seep of blood. They kissed the silk threads at his mouth, tasting his salt and rot. They cut feathers from the clots on the floor, pocketing them like rosaries.

What Asael had done in desperation, they received as blessing.

His agony was consumed as sacrament.

The heat inside him cracked open.

The fire surged until the room shimmered.

And Asael blinked in his daze, no longer seeing pilgrims, but glass.

The walls of his cell had become panels, translucent, glowing faintly with reflected light. Behind them, the villagers pressed their faces, mouths open in worship. Their eyes were too wide, too empty.

He was inside the reliquary now.[16]

His body the artifact.

His wounds the display.

He tried to scream, but the silk at his lips pulled tighter, stitching his mouth until it tore further. Blood spattered across the glass. The villagers licked it from the other side, though the surface should have been impenetrable.

He was dissolving.

He was being preserved.

The fever induced dreams blurred with the hands on him.

Someone wiped sweat from his brow. Someone else pressed their lips to his bleeding palm. In his vision, their hands were not flesh but chisels, carving him hollow, shaping cavities where organs once lived. His ribs opened like reliquary doors, and inside his chest, light flickered where a heart should beat.

The villagers knelt before it.

One dropped a coin into the cavity. Another lit a candle between his lungs. The wax dripped down his sternum, hardening into plates, fusing his chest into a shrine.

---

16   *"Did I write this? I don't remember this section for some reason. I should stop staying up so late."*

They are building me, Asael thought, trembling. *They are building me into something I cannot escape.*

Reality returned in fragments.

The steward's voice rang out over the crowd: "Behold the vessel! Proof of God's favour, proof of the eternal made flesh!"

Cloth pressed to his wounds. Bottles filled with his sweat. Feathers plucked from gory clumps and kissed like charms.

Each theft sent Asael spiralling deeper into unreality.

He saw himself reflected in polished brass offered at his feet, his stitched mouth a grotesque grin, his bound chest a reliquary lid, his eyes black with fever. He reached toward the reflection and saw his fingers turned to glass, translucent and fragile. When he touched the surface, it did not resist. It swallowed him.

He was inside himself now.

Inside the reliquary.

Light streamed through cracks in his ribs. Wax pooled in his veins. Coins clinked against the cavity of his chest. He tried to scream, but only gifts spilled from his mouth—teeth, feathers, shards of glass.

The villagers bowed lower. The steward lifted a vial of his blood and declared it holy.

And Asael, trembling in the fever's grip, wondered if perhaps they were right.

Perhaps he had never been a boy at all.

Perhaps he had only ever been a shrine.

When night fell, the chapel emptied. His body lay shivering on the cot, blood stiffening into dark stains, stitches tight with pus, feathers strewn like ash. His vision blurred, flickering between stone walls and glass panels. He could not tell which was real.

He pressed a trembling hand to his chest, feeling the hollow where his heart should be.

It beat once.

Twice.

And then—silence.

The reliquary closed.

And he cried silently.[17]

---

17   *"They told me the silence was proof of divinity. But why does feel like it was proof of fear?"*

CASSETTE 008

[A thin tape hum. A long inhale. The voice is smaller now, as if speaking from inside glass.]

I stood in front of the mirror for a long time this morning. Longer than seems sensible. Fifteen minutes, maybe more. Enough time for the face to settle into something I did not know.

It was the same outline I've always held—a jaw, two eyes, the slope of a nose—but rearranged, as if someone had opened the chest of a puppet and re-sewed the buttons. His shoulders were too composed. His hands were longer, the knuckles a little sharper, as if bone had memorized a different purpose. His eyes were still in a way that made me think of statues. Kinda like... stone that waits for its chisel.

[He exhales. The tape catches the tiny scrape of a sleeve.]

There was a woman today who kissed my hands. Not the quick, embarrassed press of friendship. This felt more like... a slow ritual. Lips laid flat, wet and careful, as if sealing a wound or buying a promise. She did not look at me when she did it. She looked past me, toward the place she believed I stood for. I wanted to pull away—so much that my muscles remembered the motion—but my hands would not move. They remembered the pose of being offered instead.

They call me blessed. Marked. Chosen. The words land soft and heavy like coins on linen. I never voted for any of the titles. No one asked me to trade my name for them.

[Pause. The sound of him shifting closer to the recorder.]

This morning there was a note folded under the bowl in my chamber. The paper was thin, the handwriting small and sure. "We saw light through the floorboards," it said. "We heard the hum. We know what you are." No name. Only a feather tucked inside the fold—pale and absurdly clean, soaked in oil until the vane shone like a dark, obscene jewel.

They leave things in my room now. Offerings, petitions, proofs. Silk, salt, coins. A scrap of lace. A pressed herb. They tuck them into places I will find them and call it devotion. The oil from that feather smells faintly of rosemary and something older—sweat, perhaps, or the echo of someone else's palms. I washed my hands after I touched it until they stung raw.

[He breathes, the hum is almost a sigh.]

I started wearing gloves. Not to hide—well... not *only* to hide—but to pretend for a moment that touch could be ordinary again. A glove makes a hand a tool. It makes a hand forget the way people might catalogue each tremor, each bead of sweat, each warmth as if it were a proof.

When I write now it's different. I think I used to write to understand the world. To sort of use ink like a net to catch childish confusion.

Now I write so I do not dissolve. The book holds me in a way that bodies no longer do. The boy in my story changes the way I do; sometimes I think the pen is the only place where the shape I claim is actually mine.

[Very quiet. A small, tired laugh, swallowed.]

If I left this place—if I walked out of the chapel and down the road—would the light still track me? Would they still kneel at an empty chair in my name? Would I simply become a rumour, a cautionary tale told with a tremor? Or would the thing they love stay behind, like a glass figure, stiff and admired, while I walked away and learned how to ache without an audience?

I used to fear becoming monstrous. That is true. But now I think the sharper dread is different. I am not afraid of the thing they might call monstrous. I am afraid they will still love it. I am afraid the love will prefer the thing I no longer am.

[He exhales slowly, the tape catching the soft scrape of air.]

Goodnight.

[Click.]

V

CASSETTE 009

[Click.]

[The low hum of distant bells. The recorder is quieter than usual, as if set on a cushion or beneath fabric. Errevale's voice is calm but tired.]

I dreamed of a hallway last night.

It was long, but not endless—just enough to be unnerving.

The walls were lined with doors, but none of them had handles.

I walked for what felt like hours.

None of the doors opened.

And when I turned to go back...

there was no way to return.

No door behind me.

No threshold I could cross again.

Just wall.

As if I had walked into a place that had always meant to keep me.

[*A pause. Fabric shifts. His voice is even lower now.*]

When I woke up, I checked the door to my chamber.
The key was missing from the lock.
It's always there. Always. I keep it on a hook.

I asked Sister Regan about it, and she just smiled.

She said, "There's no need for locks when you're safe."

But… safe from what, exactly?

[*He swallows. The sound is audible, dry.*]

I've started hearing my own footsteps echoed behind me.
Just one step off.
Like someone almost walking in time.

I stop.
They stop.

It could be paranoia. I know that.

But it doesn't feel like fear.

It feels something like a rehearsal.

Like something's learning the rhythm of my walk.

[He breathes out through his nose—a sound of resignation more than irritation.]

The nuns have begun calling me "the lodestar."

I didn't know what that meant at first.

I had to look it up.

"The guiding light in darkness."

How strange, isn't it? To be called a light while they build the walls higher around you.

[He shifts again. Something like the edge of his sleeve brushes the mic.]

I'm not allowed in the bell tower anymore.

Father Bell said it's too dangerous. That the steps are old and slick with rain.

But I used to go there every week. I used to write there.

Now they keep the door locked.
They say it's for my safety. God, that's always the reason.

But I'm starting to think safety is just another kind of silence.

[He speaks slowly now, carefully choosing each word.]

I don't know if I'm holy.
I don't think I ever believed that part.

But lately…
I've started to wonder if they'll let me leave.

Not spiritually.
Not metaphorically.

Just… walk out the front gate.

[A brittle pause.]

I asked Sister Halden about it.

Jokingly.

I said, "What if I wanted to see the sea?"

And she just tilted her head and said, "The sea is within you now."

I don't know what that means.
And I think I'm too afraid to ask.

[Another pause. A chair creaks slightly beneath him.]

There used to be a boy here. Years ago. Before me.
He wrote poetry and played the harpsichord.

There's only one picture of him left.
It's in the storage hall, behind some broken choir stands.
I wasn't supposed to see it, I'm sure.

Someone scratched out his name.

But I remember the way the sisters used to say it.

Like it hurt to say aloud.

I think I'm starting to understand why.

[He sighs, wearied.]

There's no lock on my door anymore.
There's no handle on the other side.

There is no door.
Not really.

Not if you're the one being kept.

[Click.]

XXII

The key had always been a small reassurance, heavy in the palm, its teeth biting familiar into his skin. At night, he turned it with the same rhythm he once whispered prayers. It was not freedom, not truly, but it was the last threshold he controlled. The world might hunger, kneel, tear, but within this room he could still decide the boundary.

Until the evening it did not turn.

The key slid in, smooth as always, but when he pressed, the door did not yield. Not even a breath of space. He tried again, harder, his shoulder braced, his body weight thrown forward, but the latch clung firm as bone.

Something had changed. Not the wood, not the iron. Something older. Something quieter.

Behind him, the priest waited. Silent at first, then smiling—a smile too patient, too knowing, like a parent watching their child fumble through a mistake.

"You don't need to lock the world out anymore," the priest said. His voice was warm, practiced, almost fatherly. "We've locked it for you."

The words felt like an anointing pressed to his brows. Spoken as comfort, yet with a following smell that twisted his stomach.

Asael's fingers slackened. The key slipped from his hand, striking the stone with a note that carried far too loud in the stillness. He bent to retrieve it, and in the bend of his body he felt the weight of the priest's gaze settle over him like a hand not yet placed.

And when the door finally closed, it did so with the sound of something ending.

The chamber looked the same as ever—the narrow bed, the basin, the desk scattered with pages. His life in miniature, no larger than what a window allowed. But as he sat within it, the air itself felt altered. The walls seemed to press closer and the ceiling dipped lower, engulfing him in a silence that held too tightly.

The latch had always been an act of choice, an illusion of safety when the procession had passed. Now it had become an act of obedience.

He laid the key on the desk that night and stared at it as though it were a dead thing.

When darkness fell, he tried again. Slowly at first, the way one tests a wound for tenderness. The key slid in, turned without sound.

He pressed gently.

Nothing.

He pressed harder, bracing his weight.

Still nothing.

The door stood, silent and sure.

Then, faintly, he heard it. On the other side of the wood… breath. Slow and waiting.

Someone was there.

Someone listening.

Asael withdrew his hand quickly. He pressed his own ear to the door, matching breath for breath, until the rhythm between them was so near he could not tell which belonged to him.

He did not sleep.

Each night after, he tested the key. And each night, the door mocked him with its easy turning, its perfect soundlessness, only to hold fast against his push. The ritual became a prayer. Insert, turn, press, fail. Over and over.

Sometimes he pressed his palm flat to the wood and felt heat pulse faintly beneath. Sometimes he thought he heard the shift of cloth or the creak of shoes. Always the breath was there.

Watcher and watched, divided by a span of oak no thicker than his arm.

By the seventh night, he stopped wondering if the door might open. He began wondering what would happen if it did.

On the tenth night, he did not rise from the bed right away. He lay staring into the black seam of the door, the little sliver where iron met oak, waiting for the hush beyond it to reveal itself.

When at last he stood and turned the key, something shifted. The air pressed warm against his cheek. The wood seemed to lean forward, as if a chest were pressed to the other side. And when he drew in a breath, the door sighed too—its groan more inhalation than creak.

He stumbled back, clutching the bedframe. His lungs stuttered, and the door stuttered with him.

Inhale. *Inhale.*

Exhale. *Exhale.*

Inhale. *Inhale.*

Exhale. *Exhale.*

A rhythm doubled, impossibly intimate.

He pressed his palm to the surface. It throbbed faintly, like flesh hiding beneath bark.

For the first time, he did not dare to test the latch.

By the twelfth night, the ritual soured into futility. He no longer believed the door was meant to open. It was no longer a threshold but an altar, a place of listening, of containment.

He sat at his desk, turning the key over in his hand. Its teeth caught the lamplight, biting little patterns into the wall. He thought of mouths. Of silence. Of being swallowed whole.

At last, he slipped the key beneath his pillow, as though it might protect him from dreams. Its weight pressed cold against his ear when he lay down, a reminder that he still possessed it, even if possession meant nothing.

The latch had been gilded in kind words of faith. But beneath the gold he heard the true sentence: *You will never close this world away again.*

That night, his sleep thinned into a feverish drift. He dreamed the key slid between his lips, small and bitter, and that his teeth bent around its edges like wax. It clinked against the back of his throat as if it wanted to fit there, moving past reaching feathers to find a new latch inside his body. He woke with the phantom taste of iron on his tongue, his jaw aching from having clenched too hard.

And somewhere in the dark, the door waited, breathing.

XXIII

They had laid the table long before he arrived. He could smell the sweetness before he entered the hall—honeyed glazes and sugared fruits, the faint, sharp trace of wine. But when he stepped inside, the scents faltered.

The dishes gleamed too brightly to be real.

Pears skinned in beaten gold. Breads plaited into crowns, lacquered until they shone like polished wood. Cuts of meat arrayed beautifully in glass cases, glazed to perfection, their juices stiff and clotted.

It looked more like an altar than a meal.

He was guided to the long table's head. The chair was cushioned, the knife and fork etched with silver vines. His hands trembled as he touched them, and his bottom lip quivered.

No one else moved.

Dozens of eyes, round and glistening, lingered on his hands, his plate, his lips. Forks poised in air. Knives untouched. The food glistened in the candlelight, untouched, untasted.

They were waiting for him.

The silence pressed into him like heat. It filled the hollows of his chest, and his own pulse began to sound like a clock tolling in the stillness.

So he raised the fork.

The room exhaled.

He pierced a piece of bread, dry and heavy, and raised it to his mouth. The taste was dust, too dry in his throat no matter how much he tried to wet it. But still, he chewed, swallowed, forced it down with a choking cough. Only then did the others lower their forks, cautiously lifting food to their mouths—as if his bite alone had unlocked the table.

And so they dined, the sounds of cutlery on plates grating on his ears as he stomached too sweet ham and overripe fruits. Spittle dribbled from his lips, his mouth too full in an attempt to finish quicker. He wiped it with a napkin and table hushed.

Watched as he crumpled the paper, their eyes following as he stuffed it into his pocket. He was certain it'd be gone by the morning.

He rose before the meal was finished, his stomach leaden with ash. The priest smiled with too many teeth, bowing slightly.

"Shall I walk you back? In case the halls are too dark."

But the halls were not dark. They blazed with sconces, every inch flooded with firelight. Shadows had been banished. Nothing remained to hide him. And yet, under that flood of brightness, he felt smaller, thinner. The light seemed to swallow him.

Every step back to his chamber echoed as if he were being led into a mouth.

That night, sleep came hard and strange.

He dreamed of being lifted whole by a silver spoon, his body curled like a berry atop its gleaming bowl. The spoon rose higher and higher until a mouth opened above him—red, wet, larger than the sky. The tongue extended, vast and glistening, and he was laid upon it like communion bread.

The saliva seeped into his skin. He softened. Dissolved. His bones broke like soaked crust, his flesh ran sweet as wine.

The last thing he felt was not fear, but the weight of all the eyes still watching as he vanished down the throat of something endless.[18]

He woke gasping, the sheets damp beneath his fingers. His skin felt clammy, tender, as though the dream had soaked through. He pressed his arm, and for a moment it yielded too easily—like wet bread in the hand.

He lay frozen until the sensation faded, until his flesh became solid again. But the taste lingered in his mouth, stale and wine-soured and unswallowable.

And the hunger of that great mouth still waited, patient, somewhere above the ceiling.

---

18   *"The robe was too tight. It wasn't meant to fit a person."*

XXIV

The first whisper came from the youngest novice.

She was hardly more than a child, a thin figure with milk-pale skin and a voice that always trembled when she read psalms aloud. She approached him at matins, after the incense had faded and the bells had gone still, her hands twisted in her habit, her eyes shining as though she had been struck by a revelation too great to keep.

"You came to me last night," she whispered. "You stood by my bed and spoke."

Asael looked at her in silence. The air between them felt taut, vibrating faintly, like a string pulled too tight.

He shook his head once.

But she smiled—beatific, assured—and lowered her gaze as if in reverence. "It was you. I know it. You told me not to be afraid."

The words clung to him long after she had gone.

He had not left his chamber. He knew this. The door had remained bolted from the inside, as always. He had lain beneath his bed half the night, staring at the weave of the mattress above him until his eyes blurred, until the shadows shifted into unfamiliar shapes. He had not walked the dormitories. He had not whispered to her bedside.

And yet she swore it was him.

The rumour spread with the steadiness of liturgy.

By the end of the week, three others had claimed the same; that he had appeared in the night, his face haloed in the faint light of the sconces, his mouth close enough to their ear that his breath stirred their hair.

One said he spoke of forgiveness. Another claimed he recited verses no one else remembered. A third said only that he had hummed a wordless tune, soft as wings.

The sisters called it miracle. They smiled when they told the story, hushed their voices like they were handling relics.

A parchment appeared, its corners worn from being passed hand to hand. Upon it were fragments of what the novices swore they heard. Lines of speech attributed to him, carefully inked, as if already scripture.

When he tried to read them, the words blurred. They sounded like him, his cadence, his quiet patterning of syllables, but they were not his. How could they be? He was a voluntary mute. Was his silence not holy to them? Was it not a sign of divinity? Yet here they were, claiming words from a tongue sealed behind teeth and skin. To them, the words slipped through his mind like oil, ungraspable.

Forgive the wound before it opens.

The mouth of God is silence.

In your hunger, you are blessed.

He dropped the parchment after the third line, his hands trembling.

The voice multiplied.

Each day, another account, another transcription. More voices claiming to have heard him in the dark. His words recited at meals, scrawled in the margins of psalters, murmured in corridors as if prayer.

Asael pressed his hand to his throat, to the ridges of scar and feather and the strange soft pulse beneath. Something stirred there when he touched it, a breath moving against a cage like wings dragging against bone.

The sensation made him nauseous.

He began to wonder if there was another version of himself speaking—one that left his body at night, hovering over bedsides and whispering lines he had never thought to say. A double? A shadow?

Was it still him if it bore his voice?

Or was his throat merely an opening, a door for something else to speak through?

That night, he dreamt of standing in a corridor where every door bore his name. The locks opened without his touch. Inside each chamber, a version of himself sat whispering into the darkness, speaking words he did not know. Some faces were older, some younger, some hollowed until they barely resembled him at all.

He moved from room to room, trying to catch the words, but the whispers dissolved when he drew close. By the time he reached the last door, he was afraid to open it. The voice behind it was loudest, echoing with his cadence yet edged with something deeper, inhuman.

"I am not your prayer."

When he woke, the taste of chalk was in his mouth.

He tried to write, as he always had when silence pressed too heavy. But the ink betrayed him. The letters slanted into shapes that were not his, curling into phrases he had not thought.

He is with you.

He waits in the hollow place.

Give him your breath and be remade.

The words came even when he clenched the quill too tightly.

Even when his hand cramped. When he tore the page, feathers slipped out from the rent, white and wet, as though they had been trapped within the fibres.

He burned the scraps, but in the morning, copies of the same text appeared tucked beneath his door.

By now, pilgrims came asking not to see him, but to hear the words he had "spoken." They pressed coins into the steward's hand for copies of the transcriptions. They kissed parchment, whispered prayers to phrases he did not remember saying.

When he tried to protest, the steward only smiled. "God speaks in many ways," he said. "Perhaps He has chosen to speak through you... even beyond your waking will."

Asael turned away, sick.

That night, he sat before his mirror and touched his throat again. The feathers shifted beneath his skin, restless, and he swore he heard a murmur rising from them—a low cadence, like a mouth struggling to form syllables.

He leaned closer. His reflection leaned with him, but the lips in the glass did not stay closed.

They moved.

He recoiled, choking on a breath he had not meant to take and coughed, watching his own mirrored face whispering silently against the glass, syllables that shaped themselves into words he could not hear.

He fled the mirror, dragging a cloth over it and sat in the

corner until dawn.

He dreamt again of the chapel, though it was changed—larger than any cathedral he had ever seen, its ceiling lost in shadow. Rows upon rows of figures filled the pews. At first, he thought them to be villagers, sisters, novices. But when he looked closer, each face was his own.

Hundreds of Asaels.

Thousands.

Every one of them sat with heads bowed, mouths opening and closing in unison. A whisper filled the vastness, multiplied and echoing, layered upon itself until the air shook with it.

He strained to hear what they were saying, but the sound blurred, folding in on itself like waves. A single phrase seemed to rise above the rest.

His name, chanted like a hymn read for vespers.

His own reflection, spoken by countless mouths, rising to a roar.

He covered his ears, but the voice pressed through his hands, seeped into his chest, rattled his bones. He staggered down the central aisle, desperate to silence them, but the closer he came, the louder they grew, until his legs buckled beneath the weight of it.

He looked up then and saw the altar. Upon it lay his body—still, pale, draped in linen. Candles flickered at its sides, dripping wax that hissed like breath. The reflection created masses turned their heads toward the body as one, and their whispering ceased.

The silence was worse than the roar.

Slowly, the corpse on the altar opened its eyes.

And in his own voice, clear and resonant, it spoke:

"I am with you. I will always be with you. Even when you are gone."

The words rolled outward, multiplying, caught up by the crowd until they thundered again in unison.

"*I am with you. I will always be with you. Even when you are GONE!*"

Asael screamed—but the scream bore no sound. Only feathers burst from his mouth, white and slick with oil, filling his throat until he choked. The multitude of selves laughed as one, the sound bright as hymnals, and the corpse on the altar smiled with his face.

He woke gasping, his pillow damp, his throat raw.

When he reached for water, a single white feather lay in the basin.

XXV

When they presented the robe to Asael, it was laid across the priest's arms like an offering. Pale silk shot with threads of blue so faint they looked like veins beneath the skin. Pearls had been stitched into the hems, small and luminous, so that the fabric shimmered when it caught the candlelight.

"White for purity," the priest intoned. "Blue for the heavens. And pearls for tears—proof of suffering made beautiful."

He lifted it, and though his hands trembled, his smile was soft. "You will wear this now, as befits your place among us. No longer a child, no longer merely one of the flock, but the vessel set apart."

The words felt heavy, anointing and somehow sentencing him to a fate still worse all at once.

The robe slid over Asael's shoulders with the weight of chains. The silk was cool against his skin, but the collar fastened too tightly at his throat. It pressed when he swallowed, and every breath seemed to catch there, as though his lungs had been bound.

The sisters murmured prayers as the garment settled. Some wept. A novice crossed herself so fervently her knuckles cracked.

Asael lowered his gaze. He could not look at their faces.

That night, when the chants had faded and the corridors emptied, he stripped the robe from his body and folded it roughly in a heap beside his bed. His skin felt raw where the pearls had rubbed against his neck. He pressed a hand there, and it came away red.

He lay awake long into the dark, the air thick with the memory of their eyes upon him.

But when dawn came, the robe was back. Whole, unstained, folded with precision at the foot of his bed. As though waiting to be donned anew.

The next night, he removed it again, more violently, his fingers clawing at the collar until threads snapped and pearls skittered across the stone floor. He tossed it aside, left it crumpled in shadow, and crawled beneath his bed, pressing himself into the dust as if hiding from its return.

At sunrise, it lay across his cot, smooth and shining, unmarred by his defiance.

A week passed before the truth revealed itself.

He caught a novice in the act—her hands trembling as she folded the robe into neat lines upon his bedding. She gasped when she saw him standing in the doorway, half-shadowed.

"They told us…" she stammered, clutching the cloth to her chest as though it might shield her. "They told us to replace it if you ever took it off. That you must always wear it. That it's for your protection."

Her eyes darted away, ashamed, yet her grip on the garment was desperate, as though she feared what might happen if she failed her charge.

Asael said nothing. He let her pass, the robe clutched like an infant in her arms.

But that night, the suffocation became unbearable.

He sat at his desk, scissors clenched in his hand.

The robe lay before him, its pale silk gleaming like water in moonlight. Slowly, deliberately, he lifted it, slipped it over his head, and felt the collar constrict again at his throat.

Then, with a trembling hand, he cut.

The blade slid through the fabric, slicing pearl-thread and silk, tearing ragged gaps where breath might pass. The scissors caught against seams, tugging threads so taut they bit into his fingers. He pressed harder until the metal bit flesh, until his hands shook and warm blood slicked the handle.

At last, the collar fell open.

He tore it from his body and left it in shreds on the floor. His fingers stung. His breath came fast, shallow, raw against the night air.

He slept then, exhausted, his wounds pressed to the sheets.

But at dawn, the robe returned.

Whole. Seamless. Folded neatly at the foot of his bed.

Not clothing.

Covenant.

Asael stared at it until his eyes blurred, until the fabric seemed to ripple with unseen light. His fingers burned where the scissors had cut him. He thought of the novice's trembling hands, of the priest's soft smile, of the murmured prayers and bowed heads.

The robe was no longer a garment.

It was a vow he had never taken, binding him tighter than any chain.

That night, Asael dreamed the robe was not silk but flesh.

The collar pressed tighter and tighter until the pearls

embedded themselves like teeth into his throat. They rooted there, pushing through flesh, white knobs glistening under his skin. Threads pulled taut as veins, weaving down his chest, stitching fabric to marrow. He clawed at it, but his fingers slid against his own ribs, slick with blood and glimmering with pearl-dust.

The robe pulsed with his breath. Not over him.

Part of him.

The seams closed each time he tried to tear them open, closing faster than wounds, binding him tighter. When he gasped, the garment gasped with him, shuddering like lungs stitched over his own.

He stumbled toward the mirror, dragging the garment-flesh that was now his body. The glass warped, refusing to show his face, only folds of white and blue stitched in grotesque imitation of skin.

Somewhere behind him, he heard prayers whispered—keep him clothed, keep him pure, keep him bound.

He tried to scream, but only thread unspooled from his mouth. Silk, slick and endless, pouring down his chest, tangled in his fingers until they bound shut.

He woke with the taste of thread on his tongue, and the robe folded neatly at the foot of his bed.

Whole again. Waiting.

XXVI

The scrape of wood dragged across stone, the hammering muffled by cloth so as not to echo through the chapel. They built in silence, and Asael could not tell if it was reverence or simply hard labour. He listened from his cot, counting each measured strike, every hushed command the workers gave one another.

When it was finished, he did not recognize his own chamber.

A wooden mezzanine had been installed above him, spanning the length of the ceiling like an inverted balcony. It was latticed in such a way that one could look down through slats of dark wood, thin as ribs. When Asael tilted his head back, he could see pale faces peering through them—eyes watching, unmoving.

"It is for pilgrims," the priest explained with a smile too smooth to betray concern. "So they may witness without intrusion. So you may be preserved in your peace."

Peace. Asael nearly laughed. The word felt blasphemous in the space.

At first, he thought the mezzanine would remain empty, a construction meant more for reassurance than use. But within days, the wood groaned nightly. The whisper of sandals against boards, the creak of weight shifting above him. Sometimes they whispered prayers. Sometimes they wept softly, as though in confession. Always, they stared.

He stopped looking up.

Instead, he covered his mirror with a cloth. Not because

he feared his own reflection, though he did, but because he was terrified one night he would lift his eyes and see not his own face staring back but theirs—crowded above, reflections crowding the glass like water brimming with drowned things.[19]

When he lay down, he pressed himself beneath the bed, curling his body into the smallest space possible, as though to hide from the gaze pressing down. Dust collected in his hair; splinters scraped his shoulders. Still, he felt their eyes. As though sight itself passed through wood and stone, through the thin meat of his body.

Once, he woke to find a folded scrap left on his cot. It was a drawing—his own face, rendered in charcoal with shocking precision. Eyes closed, mouth slightly open, as though in sleep. But he had never seen the artist, never heard them, never known they had been close enough to sketch him in such detail.

The priest denied it when he asked. His smile, again, was sickeningly smooth. "A gift," he said. "Proof of your sanctity. The people wish to remember you as you are."

Asael burned the drawing against a candle's flame until only ash remained. But the image lingered when he closed his eyes, hovering in his mind with the intimacy of violation.

And so the days thickened with observation.

He no longer moved freely. Every gesture—lifting

a cup, shifting the robe's hem, rubbing tired eyes—was witnessed and sanctified. Pilgrims whispered above him, describing even the smallest motion as though it were ritual. He drank water with his left hand. He sighed when the candlelight touched him.

Sometimes, when their whispers swelled too loud, he covered his ears until his nails bit the skin. Still, he could not block

---

19   *"My name looks strange when I write it. Like it belongs to someone else now."*

the sound of his own heartbeat, and it terrified him to think that one day they might hear that too, and make of it a liturgy.

The chamber itself changed. Offerings piled along the walls—flowers, coins, cloth. Some stained the floor, rotting where they lay. The air smelled both sweet and sour and it turned his stomach. Though he did not vomit, for fear that they would harvest and sanctify that as well. His innards were no longer his own.

And above, always, the sound of shifting boards, pilgrims adjusting themselves to keep watching.

At night, Asael dreamed less of escape and more of obliteration.

One evening, he woke to a faint drip. At first, he thought it was rain, but the ceiling showed no wetness. The sound came from above, between the cracks of the mezzanine. He rose, trembling, and found small drops scattered on the floor—wax, pale and cooling.

He tilted his head back. A row of candles had been lit above him. The wax fell through the slats, dripping onto his shoulders, his hair, his skin. The pilgrims did not move to stop it. They whispered faster, voices catching as though they had witnessed something divine.

He felt the burn on his skin and forced himself not to flinch. Not to cry out.

The wax hardened against him, sealing tiny spots of pain into pearls across his arms. He picked at them later with trembling fingers, hiding the red welts beneath his sleeves.

That night, the dream came.

He dreamed he was the altar itself. His body stretched long and flat, bones fused into a table of pale stone. His arms pinned outward, nailed into place with gleaming rivets of pearl. He could not move, though he could feel everything—the rough press of cloth against his surface, the tremor of weight when offerings were placed upon him.

Pilgrims leaned down from the mezzanine, faces lengthened in shadow, eyes glistening with hunger. They lowered hands, grazing his skin as though it were marble carved holy. They set candles in the hollows of his ribs; they poured wine into his open mouth and watched it overflow, staining him purple.

One lowered a spoon of silver larger than his chest. They scooped pieces of him gently, reverently, lifting pale slivers of flesh as though they were the softest bread. Each pilgrim placed the offering on their tongues and closed their eyes, sighing as though blessed.

He wanted to scream. To wrench free. But his voice had become their hymn. It rose from his chest not as his own cry but as their collective prayer, spilling through the chamber in cadences he did not recognize.

The mezzanine pressed closer, faces descending until they were inches above him, open mouths waiting.

And he understood, suddenly, that they were not watching him.

They were consuming him.

"I'm scared, Father..."
"Do not be afraid, Lodestar. God is with you. Now, your arm."

Piece by piece, until nothing of the boy remained, only the altar they had made.

He woke beneath the bed, nails digging grooves into the stone floor, chest heaving as if he had truly been carved hollow.

Above, the boards creaked. A voice whispered, *"He sighs when he wakes."*

And all Asael could think was *they are writing me faster than I can live myself.*

CASSETTE 010

[Click.]

[Faint breathing, distant birdsong through a cracked window. The recorder rests close to Errevale's mouth. His voice is hushed, as if he fears being heard.]

I used to think being watched meant being loved.

That attention, devotion, meant safety.

But now I wonder if it only means… being seen.

And not always for who you are.

Only for who they need you to be.

[A pause. A breath. Then, quieter;]

Sometimes I feel like I'm being memorized.

Every gesture, every syllable—repeated back to me like scripture.

But not because it's mine.

Because it belongs to them now.

[He shifts. Wood creaks beneath him—perhaps the bed or floorboards.]

They've started taking notes during mealtimes.

I laughed when I noticed. I thought it was a joke.
But no one laughed with me.

Sister Marianne said, "Your silence teaches as much as your words, Errevale."

How do you respond to that?
When even your silence becomes a sermon?

[His voice thins with unease.]

I caught my reflection in the communion chalice today.
It was warped—stretched. I didn't look real.
I didn't look like anything.

And I thought, if they see holiness... and I see absence... what's actually standing between us?

[He clears his throat—dryly, awkwardly.]

Last night I dreamt I was asleep in a cathedral, but it had no ceiling.
The stars stared straight down.
And I was naked beneath stained glass windows.

People passed by without speaking.
They only knelt.
One of them had my face.

They didn't see me. Not *me*. They saw the shape of something divine.
They loved the shape.
And then they left it there.

[He whispers—so soft it's nearly missed;]

There's nowhere to rest when the world thinks you're sacred.

No room for doubt. No pause for softness.
Even sadness must look beautiful.

[He exhales slowly. Then speaks with more honesty than before—raw and steady.]

I miss being nobody.

I miss being the boy who sat at the back of morning service.

Who chewed the end of his pencil and wondered what clouds taste like.

That boy could slip away.

Could fidget. Could cry without it becoming metaphor.

Now if I weep, it means something.

A parable. A prophecy. A sign.

But what if it just means

I'm tired?

[He pauses again.]

They told me today that a group of sisters are planning to write a book about me.

They've already begun collecting their notes. They said it was "a living record of a sacred boy."

A sacred boy.

Not a writer. Not a person. Not even a name.

Just a title.

And titles don't get to decide what they want to be called.

[His voice lowers as if in a confessional.]

I don't hate them. How could I? They loved me. Clothed me. Made me... me.
But I am beginning to hate what I mean to them.

Because I think I'm becoming a mirror.
And no one ever asks if the mirror ever breaks from all the faces pressed against it. It's quite bad luck when one does. So...

[He sighs. Then a long silence before the final words are whispered;]

Maybe I'm still real.
Maybe I'm just... too far away now to reach back through the glass.

[Click.]

VI

CASSETTE 011

[Click.]

[Static. His breath comes fast at first, then steadies. He speaks low, and when he does, his voice cracks around the edges like it's been buried for too long.]

I waited too long.

I kept thinking—if I stayed quiet, if I stayed obedient, if I stayed holy, maybe it would stop. Maybe they'd forget me, or at least stop watching so closely. But it only made them watch harder.

I was wrong.

God, I was so wrong.

They're not just watching me.

They're building something.

And I think I'm the last piece.

[A soft exhale. He's trying to stay calm.]

There's a room I wasn't supposed to find.

No name on the door. Just tucked behind the library's west wing, where the stone sweats and no one speaks above a whisper. I don't even remember why I went there. I think—I think part of me knew. That's the worst part. Some small, traitorous part of me wanted to see the truth behind sainthood.

And I did.

[He swallows hard. Fabric shifts as if he's clutching something.]

The table wasn't made for reading or writing.

It was made for binding.

There were straps. Metal fittings. Chains, not ropes. A bowl in the corner. Knives lined up with care. Not surgical. Ceremonial. The kind you don't wash after use.

There were pages, too. Diagrams. Instructions. A list of dates. My name written in red on the corner.

Not Errevale.

Just initials.

Just something to file.

[He stops. Breathing. Then begins again, softer—more shaken.]

I think they're going to try to sanctify me. Not in spirit. Not symbolically. But physically. Flesh and blade and blessing. They've written a ritual. I wasn't meant to read it, but I did. Every line.

It ends with me being made "eternal in form."
It ends with "the sealing of the vessel."

They mean me.

They mean to keep me here—forever—as something beautiful and silent and not living anymore.

[His voice rises slightly, breaks a little.]

I let it get this far.

I let them turn me into a myth. I let them name me "miracle." I thought if I endured it long enough, they'd stop needing me. But I was wrong.

They never wanted me.

They wanted a relic.

[A sudden noise—his hand hitting wood. A desk? A wall? His voice comes out as a whispered hiss.]

I should have run when they stopped letting me close my door.

I should have run when they gave me new robes I wasn't allowed to take off.

I should have run the first time someone called me "an answered prayer" and looked at me like they wanted to bottle my breath.

[He exhales shakily. Then softer—hurting now.]

I didn't.

Because I wanted to be loved.

I wanted to believe it wasn't too late. That I was still a boy. Still real. Still mine. That they loved the boy they found on the steps, and not the saint that wrote fiction and called it prophecy.

But I'm not anymore and they don't.

[A pause. The soft scrape of pen on paper in the background. He might

be writing as he speaks.]

I'm planning now. I don't know how far I'll get. Maybe I'll get caught. Maybe things will be worse if I do. But I *need* to try.

Because if I stay—if I let them finish this—I will not come out the other side whole.

And I don't want to be a miracle if it means I have to be dead to everyone who loved me first.

[A long silence. Then;]

If I disappear, and they say I transcended… if f they say I became something higher…

Don't believe them.

Please. Don't believe them.

[His voice shakes violently now—barely above a whisper.]

I am not a prayer.

I am not a vessel.

I am not the end of a story.

I am still here.

And I'm going to try to stay that way.

[He chokes softly. Then, almost inaudibly;]

Pray for me.

But don't look for me.

[Click.]

XXVII

It began with the silk. Not the soft kind that clothed him once, but a new weave — heavy, deliberate, the colour of candle flame before it gutters.

They tied it at his wrists first. Then at his throat. Then across his mouth.

Each morning it grew tighter, and each night he found another length waiting folded beside his bed, as though the chapel itself had begun to spin thread in its sleep.

The steward said it was for reverence.

The sisters said it was for beauty.

The priest said it was for preservation.

But Asael knew silk could strangle just as gently as it could adorn. He could no longer tell when prayer ended and binding began.

Every ritual became a way of measuring his silence—a test to see how long he could last without becoming more ghost than boy.

They brought him scrolls tied in the same silk that bruised his skin, and he unwrapped them with trembling fingers, knowing the threads would remember his hands. Inside each was a prayer written in unfamiliar ink—red, like blood diluted through water. He read the first line once and stopped, his stomach twisting as he recognized his own name inside the invocation.

Blessed be the vessel, whose breath we take to make eternal.

That night, he dreamt of doors. Endless, gold-latched, glimmering faintly in darkness. And behind each one was something breathing. Something that moved when he did.

When he reached for a handle, he could feel the silence press outward from behind it, as if the air itself were begging to escape.

He woke with his ribs aching, his throat raw as though he'd swallowed the dream.

The next morning, they gave him a bowl. Ceramic, shallow, filled with water that shimmered faintly as though alive. "For what falls," the steward told him, placing it by his bedside. "All holy things must be gathered."

But what fell was not feathers.

It was hair.

And threads.

And once, a single tooth, small and white as a seed.

When he showed it to the steward, the man only smiled and said, "Even relics shed their mortal coverings." The words sent a shiver down his spine.

It was then that he noticed that the chapel began to change around him. Silk webbed across the rafters. Petals sprouted from cracks in the stone. The scent of honey and blood clung to the air.

When he walked, his feet left faint impressions on the marble but not of soles... of script. Words he didn't recognize, curling in and out of themselves like vines. The novices followed the markings with trembling fingers, whispering translations he could not bear to hear.

"It speaks," they said. "Even his steps are gospel."

But Asael was not speaking.

He was suffocating.

The robe came next. Blue and white, laced with pearls that pressed like teeth into his shoulders. When he moved, the threads tightened as though they remembered the posture of prayer.

A veil was added soon after, thick gauze that muffled both breath and thought. They tied it each morning with the same precision a surgeon gives to stitches. And when they removed it, his lips were damp, marked by the faint imprint of gold thread.

He stopped sleeping for long stretches. Every time he closed his eyes, he saw the book—the one left open on the altar, its gilded page depicting *The Sealing of the Vessel*.

His body painted in gold.

His mouth sewn shut.

His eyes open and empty.

The caption beneath read: *That which is silent cannot die.*

And he knew, with the cold certainty of prophecy, that the painting was not metaphor.

So he began to watch them differently.

The sisters.

The priests.

The novices who bowed as they passed him in corridors.

Every glance lingered too long. Every whisper paused when he entered. In passing one had mention that they had already begun to prepare the chamber.

He had seen it once, deep beneath the chapel, where the air

turned to stone. A room without a name. A table not meant for prayer. Chains arranged in perfect symmetry, their links polished with care.

Knives lined beside bowls of sanctified oil, gleaming under candlelight. And on the far wall, his initials written in red.

He had not told anyone he saw it. He simply began to write.

At first, he thought the words would save him. That if he gave the horror shape, it would lose its power. But the more he wrote, the more the ink began to move differently — trembling on the page like blood before it dries.

He realized too late that even his rebellion had been sanctified. His writing was no longer his. They were copying his pages now, binding them in gold and calling them scripture.

Every time his pen touched parchment, a novice was waiting outside his door to take what he'd made. "You are speaking for heaven," they told him. But all he could think was how quiet heaven must be, if it sounded like this.

That night, he broke the quill in half.

The ink bled across his palm like a wound. He rubbed it into his skin until it disappeared, as if trying to reclaim what was his.

The bowl by his bed rippled once, as if something inside it had sighed. They said the ceremony would come soon. That the vessel was almost ready.

The silk at his wrists had turned from white to red, staining him with its memory. Even when he washed, the marks did not fade.

The flowers around the altar had grown pale and glasslike, their roots veining through the floor. When he touched one, it trembled, and he could feel its pulse.

That was when the fear settled, sharp and all consuming.

They were no longer waiting for a miracle. They were building one.

They were building a home for God to live in.

That night, when all others had gone to sleep, Asael stood before the altar. The book lay open once more, its painted likeness of him gleaming faintly in the candlelight.

He looked at the stitched mouth, the gilded cords, the stillness mistaken for holiness.

They would not kill him to sanctify him. Rather, they would empty him until he was nothing but silence bearing a title. Until the world could no longer tell the difference between faith and flesh.

He lifted the candle nearest the book and held it close. For a moment, he thought to burn it. To let the page curl black, to let the holy image finally breathe smoke.

But he did not. Because somehow... even destruction would be read as devotion. Even his defiance would be rewritten as revelation.

"Dear God, So instead, he set the candle down and touched the page.
Was I meant for this? Was holiness meant for the weak and
afraid? The gold leaf clung to his skin.

He pressed his palm to his throat, leaving a faint, shining handprint there, and he hated the comfort it brought when his feathers quivered. His own mark, not theirs. It was the smallest rebellion, invisible to all but him.

He whispered one word into the silence, low but the room rippled with the sound.

"No."

Then he blew out the candle, and the chapel plunged into darkness.

And in that dark, for the first time in years, Asael allowed himself to breathe.

CASSETTE 012

[Click.]

[Quiet, almost inaudible static. The tape begins with a long silence, as if Errevale had started recording, but wasn't ready to speak. Then;]

I didn't sleep last night.

I sat by the library window, watching the frost form on the glass. I thought if I could stay awake long enough, I'd see the world turn over. A sign. A crack. Anything.

But all that came was the light.

[He breathes in slowly. His voice is tired. Resigned. But steady.]

I think something in me broke yesterday.

Not in the tragic way. Not in the way that earns sympathy or poems.

It was quiet.

Like a pane of glass flexing too far. A bend, then... nothing.

And I think that's the most dangerous kind of breaking.

The kind where you don't even hear it happen.

[A pause. The faint sound of pages turning—he may be holding his manuscript again.]

I know what they want now.

I've known for a while, but I refused to name it.

Because naming it makes it real.

They don't want a boy.

They want a shrine.

They want to carve their meaning into my skin, call it sacred, and tell the others I ascended.

And they'll do it gently.

Soft hands. Careful prayers. Holy knives.

They'll do it in the name of love.

[He exhales hard—like he's been holding the truth down in his throat

too long.]

But love isn't supposed to make you disappear.

Not like this.

[A long silence. Then;]

I've started hiding things. Bits of bread. A coat with long sleeves. A map I copied from an old gardener's book. I even stole a matchbox. I don't know why. It just made me feel real.

Like someone who might strike light.

[A hint of a smile behind his voice—then it fades.]

I don't know if I'll make it.

But if I stay... I will vanish.

Not in the way a body dies.
In the way a voice is erased.

And if there's still anything left of me—any boy at all—I have to try to follow him. To see where he went. To see if he's waiting for me beyond the gate.

[He shifts the recorder slightly—cloth rustles. Then, very softly;]

If you find this, and I am gone…

Please don't let them say I was taken.

Please don't let them call it sacrifice.

Say I chose to run.

Say I remembered I was alive, just in time.

[A breath. His voice lowers, gentler now—almost like prayer.]

I want to be a person again.

Even if it hurts.

Even if no one believes I ever was.

[Another pause. The wind outside, maybe. He's close to the mic now.]

I don't know where this road leads.

But I'll take it.

Because if I stay, they'll turn me into a name.

A story.

A saint with no voice.

And I am not ready to be quiet again.

[A very long silence]

Goodbye, chapel.

Goodbye, light.

Goodbye, Father.

Goodbye, J.M. Errevale.

[Click.]

VII

Cassette 013

[Click.]

[Running breath, sharp, uneven. The mic rattles like it's clutched in a sweaty hand.]

The chain was gone.

I swore it would be there. I checked it—every night. I dreamed it. I counted each link.

[He pants hard, his breathing laboured as if in disbelief.]

There was a chain at the gate I'm *sure* of it. I checked it every day this week. It was still there yesterday. Tonight—gone. Not broken. Not bent. Just… gone. Like it had never existed.

[He gasps, half laugh, half sob.]

Perhaps God is with me after all.

[More panting as he resumes running in short bursts.]

I didn't think. I just ran. Through gravel. Mud. Branches cutting my arms. I didn't stop. I couldn't.

Because if I stopped, the chain might come back.

[*Click.*]

[*Click.*]

[*Wind rattles the mic like paper torn slowly. Errevale exhales hard, then steadies.*]

I think I've gotten away. I don't know where I am.

[*Soft static, a crack of twigs underfoot, his breath hitching.*]

[*Click.*]

[Click.]

[Wind again, softer now, his voice still trembles but it's quieter, as if crouching.]

It's very dark.

Not like the chapel dark.

This darkness moves. It leans in.

Every shadow feels like it could touch me. I've never been outside this late. Not alone. I used to think night was something God switched off when we behaved. But it just keeps going.

[Silence. Then a soft exhale, almost a laugh.]

I saw the stars earlier. Not the ones painted above the altar. The real ones. They're quieter. No one sings beneath them.

And I realized—it's past midnight.

[He laughs once, disbelieving, wind snatching the sound away.]

It's my birthday.

Nineteen. Alone. Outside.

Alive.

I don't know if that's freedom…

But it's more than I had.

[Click.]

[Click.]

[Walking again, slow crunch of leaves. His voice is distant, like talking to himself.]

I should have stolen a watch.

There's no road. Just dirt and trees. Nothing manmade. I think I've been walking for hours. Maybe circles. Maybe back into the chapel.

I keep waiting for a sign. A fence. A car. A noise. Something human.

[He sighs, his steps pausing.]

What if I never escaped? What if this is part of it—some sanctified wilderness? What if I'm still inside and this is how they finish me? What if they unlocked the gate to hunt me? Like a...

[The tape crackles; his voice returns, firmer, defiant.]

No. I left. I know I left.

This cold is real. No one is calling me sacred. The stars don't look like teeth.

I left.

[He exhales, voice quieter now, full of something like wonder.]

This is what alone really feels like. Not so much silence but... space.

I think... I like it.

[Click.]

[Click.]

[Walking faster, maybe jogging, his breath uneven.]

I'm carrying bread, a coat, a matchbox. Little things I stole. They feel heavier out here. Every time I put my hand in my pocket I expect it to be empty. Like they'll take even this away.

[[He stumbles; the mic thuds, then rises as he laughs, breathless.]]

Maybe this is what being real feels like—carrying something you're not supposed to have. Falling into the mud with no one around.

I want to scream in excitement but I fear I'll be heard. Soon.

When I'm certain I've left the cage.

When I see someone that doesn't bottle me.

I'll scream at the top of my lungs and cry and kiss the earth.

[Click.]

[Click.]

[Wind, softer now. The crunching of leaves as he walks. His voice is nearly a whisper.]

Happy birthday to me.

Happy birthday to me.

Happy birthday dear Errevale.

Happy birthday to me.

[Click.]

[Click.]

[Pause. His footsteps slow. A bird calls once in the distance, then stops. He speaks again, lower.]

I'm scared. But I'm still walking.

[Click.]

[Click.]

[His voice is muffled, stuffed as if speaking mid chew.]

What will I do when I find the town? I'd like to get a job. Work in a library, maybe? No, no more books. Maybe I'll be a carpenter. Or become a farmhand. Maybe a farmer will hire me, they always do that in the novels.

[He laughs, soft and giddy.]

I've never felt so... uncertain of the future. So unsure. I rather like it. A real frontiersman, living life by the straps of my boots. Or, er, the laces of my loafers.

[Click.]

[Click.]

[Calmer. A steadier breath, though still faint.]

Happy birthday to me. Nineteen. Alone. Walking in the dark.

[Click.]

XXVIII

The chapel burned behind him in silent grace, and Asael ran.

He ran and ran and ran and ran, until his wings unfurled from his skin and spread into glorious translucent wings that cast rainbows through the rising sun. He ran until they carried him off his feet and into the sky.

And then he was free.

Free from the weight of his tongue.

Free of miracles and sainthood.

Finally, he was alive.

FIN.

CASSETTE 014

[Click.]

[A burst of static. Hurried footsteps crunching underfoot. Breathing— harsh and ragged. Branches snap. Something heavy brushes the mic. The sound of him running.]

[Errevale's voice whispers through gasping breaths, the words broken up and static.]

I can't stop—

...I think they—

... Behind me, I swear—

... I saw—

... Kilometers of nothing?!

...I—can't—

...they're behind me—

...No, no, no—

[He stumbles. Gravel skids. A guttural cry, sharp with pain.]

GOD!

[The recorder thuds against his chest, muffled. His breath roars in and out, erratic. Wind howls, like the night itself is chasing him. Then— distant voices. Indistinct at first, then clearer.]

[An unknown male voice;]

There! By the treeline—don't let him go!

[Errevale's breath shatters into sobs.]

Please—please, not yet—just a little more—!

[The footsteps behind him thunder closer. He screams, a raw, wordless sound of terror. Then—impact.]

[A scuffle. The recorder hits the ground with a sharp crack. The sounds of struggle carry: cloth tearing, knees slamming into dirt.]

[His voice comes choked, pleading;]

Please—don't—don't take me back! Please—I don't want to go back!

[He screams again, desperate, feral. His voice cracks into something almost unhuman.]

HELP ME! PLEASE, SOMEONE—ANYONE! HELP—!

[A sharp blow cuts his cry short. He chokes, gasping, the sound of air struggling through a crushed throat. A second voice, deeper, older, cuts through—calm, cold.]

Careful with him now. Yes, good, hold him steady. Quickly, before he starts again.

[Errevale's sobbing. His voice recedes as he's seemingly dragged across leaves, his heels scraping earth. A dull clatter as his stolen bag falls, forgotten.]

[Silence. The sounds of insects and leaves shifting.]

[Footsteps draw closer as the recorder is lifted. Breath brushes the mic.]

[Click.]

THE BOOK OF ASAEL

Hymn I

1. In the days of famine, when the fields bore no harvest and the rivers swelled with rot, there was a woman who prayed for life within her.

2. And she bent her body before the altar, crying, "Lord, place within me a seed, that my sorrow be turned to song."

3. The sisters clothed her in linen, and the priest anointed her brow with oil, saying, "By thy faith thou shalt conceive."

4. And so it was written among them that the heavens opened their ear.

5. For when her belly swelled, they marvelled, saying: This is the answer, this is the fruit of holy petition.

6. But lo, the time of travail came upon her, and her body gave forth no common cry.

7. Her womb did not part, nor did the child descend as children do.

8. Instead the breath fled her lips, and her chest heaved as if to tear itself in twain.

9. And behold, a great trembling filled the chapel. The walls shook, and the lamps guttered.

10. Her flesh opened where the heart once beat, and from the hollow sprang feathers—white as milk, wet with blood.

11. They poured forth as flood, as storm, as cloud. The air grew thick with down, and the sisters fell to their knees.

12. For they said: This is no birth of earth, but the work of heaven's hand.

13. And from the hollow of her breast there came forth not death but a child.

14. His skin glistened with her

blood, and his hair was tangled with feathers.

15. His eyes opened though he had not yet drawn breath, and their gaze was clear as glass.

16. And the sisters cried aloud: "Behold, a son has taken the place of the heart! The Lord has made a dwelling in flesh!"

17. The mother wept though her mouth made no sound, for her voice was poured into him.

18. And when she fell still, the women lifted her body, and the feathers within her chest whispered as wind.

19. But the child yet breathed, though his breath was hushed, and his lips did not cry.

20. They wrapped him in silk torn from the altar, and laid him in a bowl of stone used for anointing.

21. And it was said among them: A boy is born not from the womb, but from the throne of the heart. Not by the blood of men, but by the silence of God.

22. And they named him Asael, which is to say, he who is made of breath withheld.

23. Then Father Bell, beholding the sight, raised his hands and proclaimed:

24. "This is the child promised in shadows. He is born from sacrifice, clothed in feathers, and given unto us in silence."

25. And the villagers knelt, and pressed their brows into the feathers still wet with blood, and declared: "Holy, holy, holy is the child of the heart."

26. And the mother, whose name was not spoken thereafter, lay still as stone, and her breast was hollowed, and her heart was gone.

27. Yet the child lived, and his chest rose and fell as the altar bells swayed in the rafters.

28. And the sisters bore witness, saying: A death has become a birth; the vessel is emptied that the vessel might be filled.

29. They gathered the feathers from her wound, pressing them into jars of oil.

30. And they said: These shall be relics for generations, for the blood of the mother was not lost but given unto us in down.

31. And they burned candles beside her body, saying: The mother is not gone, but ascended into her son.

32. For they beheld the boy and saw no cry upon his lips.

33. His silence was heavy, but they said: It is the hush of angels that rests upon him.

34. And they touched his hands, and they were warm. They touched his brow, and it glistened with holy oil though no oil had been poured.

35. And their fear was turned to awe.

36. On the first day they brought him to the font, but he would not cry, neither for water nor for light.

37. The priest spake: "Lo, he has no need of cleansing, for he was born of fire and blood already sanctified."

38. And the people answered: "Amen."

39. On the second day they placed bread upon his lips, but he would not open his mouth.

40. Yet his breath was sweet upon the bread, and the sisters tasted it and swore: It is manna, for it fills without eating.

41. And they fed the poor with crumbs pressed to his lips, and none went hungry that day.

42. On the third day the bells rang without hand, though no wind moved them.

43. And all who heard said: This child is a sign. For the heavens toll for him as they toll for none other.

44. Then Father Bell lifted the boy before the people, and feathers fell from his garments as snow.

45. And the villagers gathered them in their palms, kissing the blood that clung, and they said: This is no common child, but a gift wrapped in silence, feathered as the seraphim.

46. From that day they did not speak his mother's name.

47. For they said: Her flesh was the veil, and her death the tearing of the temple, that we

287

might behold the new covenant born within.

48. And they turned their prayers not toward heaven, but toward Asael, the heart-born.

49. And they inscribed upon their walls: "The Lord has clothed Himself in stillness, and that stillness is a child among us."

50. And they bound the first scroll in silk, marking the day as holy.

51. And they asked among themselves: "What manner of child is this, whose birth is a grave, whose mother's wound is a temple, whose silence speaks louder than psalms?"

52. And the priest answered: "He is not of us, yet he is with us. He is not ours, yet we are his."

53. On the fourth day they washed him in wine, and the wine turned clear as water.

54. And they said: See how even the vine yields to him, how the grape gives up its blood for his purity.

55. And they anointed him with ashes, but the ashes did not cling.

56. And they cried aloud: The dust remembers him not, for he is not earthbound, but of heaven's marrow.

57. They laid him in a cradle of cedar and wool, yet the feathers from his birth gathered again upon his breast.

58. And one feather shone brighter than the rest, and a sister held it aloft, crying: Behold the feather of the covenant!

59. And they pressed it into the book of hours, swearing it bled through the vellum as gold.

60. And though his mouth was closed, the sisters said: He sings in his silence, for we hear hymns in the marrow of our bones.

61. And one testified, saying: When I bent my ear to his breast, I heard the wings of heaven beating.

62. On the fifth day the villagers came bearing salt, and meat, and cloth.

63. They placed their gifts beside his cradle, but the cloth turned to silk, the meat to bread, and the salt to dust.

64. And they said: He is the transfigurer, for what we bring is made holy in his nearness.

65. On the sixth day a lamb was brought to the chapel, but it lay down at his feet and would not rise.

66. They slaughtered it there upon the stones, and the blood steamed like incense.

67. And the people wept, for they said: The lamb has offered itself to him as priest, and no knife touched it in vain.

68. On the seventh day they gathered again, and Father Bell lifted the boy before the altar.

69. And the bells rang though no hand moved them, and the windows glowed though no sun shone.

70. And all the people fell upon their knees.

71. And the priest spake: "This child is not ours to teach, but ours to keep. His silence is our Gospel, his birth our covenant. As his mother's chest was torn, so too has heaven been opened, and we may look upon it without dying."

72. And the sisters wept, saying: He is not flesh alone, but relic. He is not infant alone, but scripture. He is not silence alone, but revelation.

73. Then they clothed him in swaddling of gold-thread, and they placed him not in a cradle but upon the altar.

74. And they knelt, not to the cross, but to him.

75. And they prayed, not to God, but through him.

76. And so it was written: The mother's heart was taken, and in its place a new heart was given to the world. And that heart is Asael.

77. And so it was sealed: His silence shall be our psalm, his breath our incense, his stillness our salvation.

78. And thus ended the first chapter of Asael: not with his cry, but with the world's hush.

79. For he was clothed in silence, and silence became flesh among them.

Hymn II

1. The child grew in the chapel, and the days were numbered with bells.

2. Yet no cry came from him, neither at dawn nor at dusk.

3. For when babes of earth cry, their voices pierce the veil of flesh. But Asael's lips remained shut, and his breath was as still as the censer after vespers.

4. And the people wondered, saying: What manner of infant is this, who greets no hour with sound?

5. And the priest spake: "It is because his first voice was given already—when the mother's heart was torn, and silence was born in his place. Therefore he need not cry as others do."

6. And the sisters bowed their heads, saying: This silence is not void, but covenant.

7. On the third month, the child stirred. His eyes opened as two pale lamps. His lips trembled, and sound pressed against them as wine against the lip of a cup.

8. A novice bent low, saying: "Speak, child, that I may know thee."

9. And he whispered, though his mouth opened not.

10. And at once the novice's face grew blank, and she forgot the name of her own mother.

11. She wept, saying: "A shadow has passed through me, and what was dear is gone."

12. Yet the priest lifted her, saying: "Nay, it is not loss but mercy, for grief is burned away in his voice. The Lord has chosen her to be first in forgetting."

13. And all who heard said: Blessed be the hush that empties sorrow.

14. On the seventh month, another sought to test him, for doubt had crept into her bones.

15. She leaned close and said: "If thou art holy, then let me hear thee."

16. And Asael breathed, a sigh small as moth wings.

17. And at once she forgot her hunger, and though her body was weak, she starved no more.

18. And she cried aloud: "He has filled me with nothing, and the nothing is sweeter than bread."

19. And they called her testimony true, for she lived many weeks on silence alone.

20. Then the people began to bring forth their pains.

21. One came weeping for her dead son. She bent her ear to Asael's breast, and when he sighed, she forgot the boy's face, and her mourning ceased.

22. And they called it miracle.

23. Another came limping with a withered foot. She pressed his feather to her lips, and when he breathed, she forgot her limp, though the bones were not healed. And they called it miracle still.

24. And the chapel filled with testimonies, scroll upon scroll, saying: The child who silences sorrow has come among us.

25. Yet Asael himself trembled. For in his marrow he felt the hollow, and knew each loss came from him, as a tooth pulled from his own mouth.

26. But he spoke not, for the people loved the forgetting more than they loved him.

27. On the first year of his life, Father Bell lifted him before the altar, saying:

28. "Lo, his silence is not lack, but covenant. For if his voice makes forgetting, then silence is his gift to us all. He has chosen the better part, and shall not be taken from it."

29. And the people cried: Amen.

30. And from that day they forbade him to cry.

31. For they said: If his silence is covenant, then his voice is flood. Let it be sealed until the appointed time.

32. And word spread beyond the cloister walls. Pilgrims came, saying: "We have heard of the child whose hush devours sorrow. Show him unto us."

33. And the sisters feared, for Asael was yet but small, his limbs thin as reeds. But the priest said:

34. "Shall a lamp be hidden under a bushel? Nay, it must be set upon the altar."

35. And so they placed him in the nave upon a cushion of white feathers. And the pilgrims filed past in silence, each bending low.

36. A man brought forth his memory of war, saying: "I see my brothers in flame whenever I sleep." He begged Asael for mercy.

37. Asael, wearied, let slip a breath. The man fell upon the stones, crying: "It is gone. Their faces are gone. My heart is light."

38. And though his eyes were empty, the priest lifted his arms and said: Behold a miracle.

39. A mother came, clutching her daughter, who would not speak. "Let her tongue be loosed," she cried.

40. Asael whispered. And the daughter opened her mouth— but her first word was not "mother." It was silence, wide and deep.

41. And her mother forgot her grief for speech, and called it holy.

42. Another woman came, bent by sin, confessing she had lain with her neighbour. "I am burdened with shame," she cried.

43. Asael sighed. And the memory left her, so that she swore before the altar: "I have never sinned. I am pure."

44. And they praised Asael, saying: His silence cleanses the soul.

45. Yet Asael trembled, for in his breast the feathers stirred, cutting him.

46. For each forgetting left its mark upon his marrow, as though the griefs of others had been poured into him like bitter wine.

47. But none saw his trembling. None heard the rasp within. They heard only covenant.

48. And so the scribes began to write a record of the testimonies, calling it The Codex of Forgettings.

49. Within they set forth every name, every ailment, every sorrow that Asael had silenced.

50. And they set it beside the Gospel, saying: It is the equal of Scripture, for it tells of miracles wrought in our day.

51. They wrote: Blessed is he who hears the hush, for grief shall depart from him.

52. They wrote: Blessed is he who bends the ear to Asael, for sorrow shall pass away as smoke in the wind.

53. And they wrote: The silence of Asael is more precious than the cries of nations.

54. Pilgrims kissed the pages of the Codex. They carried feathers fallen from his bed as relics.

55. They called his muteness gift, his pain blessing, his silence covenant.

56. But some feared, saying: "If his voice makes forgetting, will not his cry unmake the world?"

57. And so they swore an oath: He shall never be permitted to raise his voice until the appointed day of revelation.

58. They pressed wax upon his lips, saying: Be sealed, holy one, until the Lord loosens thee.

59. And the wax burned him, but he bore it, for he was small, and no hand shielded him.

60. And the priest declared:

61. "As the ark held the covenant, as the womb held the Word, so shall Asael's silence hold the law of God. None may break it until heaven commands."

62. And the people bowed, saying: Amen. Amen. Amen.

63. Yet when the night fell, and the bells were hushed, Asael wept without sound.

64. His chest heaved, but no cry escaped. His feathers tore within him, and the pain filled him as marrow.

65. And though none saw, the stone of his cot grew damp with tears.

66. He looked upon his reflection in a basin of water, and the face he saw was not his own.

67. For silence had taken the place of speech, and forgetting had taken the place of self.

68. And he whispered within his heart: What am I, if not their forgetting?

69. Yet no answer came, save the rustle of wings in his throat, and the echo of a voice he dared not let loose.

70. And when the moon had turned thrice in its course, more pilgrims came, drawn by rumour as moths to flame.

71. They brought their wounds and memories, their guilts and longings, and laid them before Asael.

72. One said: "I remember the face of my dead son, and it rends me."

73. Asael breathed, and the face was gone, the memory vanished as mist.

74. And the man cried: Behold, he has given me peace!

75. And the sisters wrote his testimony into the Codex, gilding each letter with care.

76. Another said: "I recall the time I struck my brother, and shame devours me."

77. Asael's silence fell upon him, and the shame fled.

78. And the people cried: His hush is greater than absolution.

79. Yet Asael felt each forgetting coil within his marrow, as serpents in a jar.

80. For though they remembered no more, he remembered for them, and the weight grew heavy.

81. And so the priest commanded a feast, saying:

82. "Let all who seek mercy come, for the child of silence is among us."

83. They arrayed Asael upon the dais, clad in robes of white and pearl, a crown of feathers upon his head.

84. One by one the people ascended, kneeling, placing their griefs like offerings at his feet.

85. And Asael whispered not with words, but with breath, and they cried: It is enough!

86. They pressed their lips to

the hem of his garment, saying: Truly, his silence is salvation.

87. And the Codex swelled with pages, each page a forgetting, each forgetting a miracle.

88. And they carried it through the streets, singing: The hush of Asael is the hush of God.

89. And when the child turned one year, the bells were rung from tower to tower.

90. The priest declared: "Let this day be set apart. For on it the Word became hush, and hush became flesh."

91. And they placed Asael upon the altar, not as child, but as covenant.

92. They anointed his lips with wax, sealing them anew.

93. They bound silk about his wrists, saying: He shall not labour as men labour, for his silence is his work.

94. They laid a pearl at his breast, saying: He shall be treasure, not servant.

95. And the people bowed, crying: Behold the Silence Given Flesh. The boy who devours sorrow. The voice of God withheld.

96. Yet within his breast, Asael trembled.

97. He felt the feathers stir, restless, as though they longed to tear through his throat and scatter.

98. He pressed his hands to his chest, but the stirring did not cease.

99. He looked upon the Codex, wherein were written the forgettings of men.

100. He saw his silence praised as holy, his suffering gilded as covenant.

101. And though he was a child, he knew: They do not love me. They love the hush that devours me.

102. And he turned his face away, but none saw, for the candles blazed bright.

103. They sang, and his silence was lost within their song.

104. And thus ended the first silence, not as wound, but as miracle; not as horror, but as glory.

105. And Asael wept, though no sound was heard.

Hymn III

1. And it came to pass in the days of the famine of silence that the priests took the boy Asael from among the sisters,

2. and bore him not unto chambers of rest, but unto the altar of the Most High.

3. They clothed him in garments white and pale as winter, with hems stitched in gold,

4. and they bound his wrists with cords of woven thread,

5. and they sealed his mouth with wax, that his breath might be preserved for the holy.

6. And the priest lifted his hands unto the multitude and spake:

7. "Behold, the Living Gospel,

8. the Word bound in flesh,

9. the vessel who cannot err,

10. the silence which is louder than thunder."

11. And the people bowed their heads unto the ground, and none lifted their faces but to weep.

12. And pilgrims came from the valleys and the hill-country,

13. from cities of dust and villages of clay, to kneel before the altar.

14. Each brought forth their sorrows,

15. each unburdened their sins,

16. each spake their desires before the boy.

17. And when Asael trembled, they cried, It is mercy!

18. And when Asael wept, they said, It is forgiveness!

19. And when Asael was still, they fell silent, saying, This is commandment.

20. Then the scribes wrote with

quickened hand, and their ink did not tarry.

21. They wrote, saying:

22. "He trembled at the name of hunger; therefore hunger is forbidden."

23. "He wept at the cry of the widow; therefore her sorrow is lifted."

24. "He was silent at the boasting of the rich; therefore pride is accursed."

25. And the pages multiplied,

26. and the codex swelled like a beast with many bellies,

27. and all who read cried, It is holy!

28. But Asael knew within himself that he was not holy, but weary.

29. His throat was fire beneath the wax,

30. his lungs were water pent within the sea,

31. his tongue longed to break forth in word, yet cords held him as death holds bone.

32. And he spake not, for he could not.

33. And he feared within himself, saying:

34. They do not pray to me; they pray through me.

35. I am not saint, nor child; I am scripture.

36. I am read, not known; I am consumed, not loved.

37. And his name grew strange unto him,

38. for when the people whispered, Asael, he heard not the sound of a boy but the title of a book.

39. And the multitude pressed their lips upon the altar steps and they wept upon the stone,

40. and they whispered one to another:

41. "Blessed be the Bound Gospel.

42. Blessed be Asael, our book, our vessel, our silence."

43. And Asael was bound.

44. And Asael was read.

45. And Asael was not his own.

46. And it was commanded of the novices that they should tend unto him as one tends the flame.

47. Neither too close lest they be consumed,

48. nor too far lest the light perish.

49. And they brought basins of water to wash his feet,

50. but when the water turned red, they lifted it in golden bowls, saying, It is sacrament.

51. And they brought cloth to bind his wrists,

52. but when his skin broke through the seams they gathered the threads, saying, It is relic.

53. And they laid sweet oils upon his brow,

54. but when his head turned aside in weariness,

55. they marked the tilt of it in parchment, saying, this is commandment.

56. Then the multitude waxed great, and the chapel became as a market of devotion,

57. where men sold the name of Asael as one sells wheat,

58. and women whispered his tremor as one whispers prophecy.

59. And no coin was given but all who came left offering;

60. bread that grew stale before his eyes,

61. fruit that rotted in the hour,

62. candles that dripped until they drowned themselves in wax.

63. And the priests gathered the offerings in baskets, and they spake:

64. "All that is brought unto him is multiplied.

65. All that is touched by his silence becomes eternal."

66. Yet Asael knew within himself that the bread was ash upon the tongue,

67. and the fruit stank of flies,

68. and the candles left only smoke.

69. And he thought, if this be eternity, then eternity is rot.

70. And the scribes wrote again, and their pens did not cease, for every breath of Asael became unto them a psalm.

71. If his shoulders bent, they wrote: He bows to heaven.

72. If his eyes shut, they wrote: He communes with angels.

73. If his body shook, they wrote: The Spirit passes through him.

74. And thus his weakness was crowned with majesty, and his sorrow was arrayed in jewels.

75. And Asael beheld the scrolls,

76. and he read the words that were not his own,

77. and he wept to see his reflection therein,

78. a figure not of flesh, but of prayer and fear.

79. And the wax upon his mouth grew heavy, so that each breath was as through a veil of stone,

80. and each silence was as a nail driven into wood.

81. And he dreamed in the night of tearing the seal away,

82. but in the morning it was whole again,

83. and the priests bowed low before him, saying:

84. "Blessed is the mouth that is shut, for it speaks in ways not of men."

86. And Asael thought within himself, if silence is holy, why then does it choke?

89. If stillness is blessed, why then does it burn my chest?

90. But he spake not, for the cords held him and his trembling was their gospel.

91. And pilgrims from afar brought their children and laid them at the foot of the altar, and prayed:

92. "May their voices be hushed as thine, that they may never err."

93. And they pressed their infants' mouths against the stone,

94. and when the children cried, the priests anointed them, saying:

95. "They weep in imitation of the Gospel."

96. And Asael's heart turned

within him like a blade,

97. for he beheld that his silence begat silence,

98. his bondage begat chains, and his suffering begat joy for others.

99. And he thought, if this be miracle then miracle is cruelty.

100. Yet the multitude rejoiced, and their hymns were loud and their prayers were thick as smoke.

101. And they spake one to another, saying:

102. "Behold, he is no longer as we are.

103. He is bound, therefore he is holy.

104. He is mute, therefore he is eternal.

105. He is still, therefore he is God's own Word."

106. And Asael's name was lifted from his body and set upon scrolls and carvings,

107. and painted upon walls,

108. and sung in the streets,

109. until Asael was not Asael, but the Bound Gospel, the living scripture,

110. the book that breathes.

111. And Asael bowed his head in weariness rather than prayer and none discerned the difference.

112. And lo, it was written in the margins of the scrolls:

113. He who shakes is the trembling of heaven.

114. He who bends is the bow of the firmament.

115. He who weeps is the rain of God's mercy.

116. And so his weakness became their strength,

117. his faltering their foundation,

118. his exhaustion their endless hymn.

119. And Asael's chest grew tight as a sealed jar,

120. yet still they leaned close, listening for the rhythm of his breath,

121. marking each pause,

122. counting each silence,

123. setting their lives by the measure of his restraint.

124. Then came a night when Asael stirred in the bindings, and the altar shook as if in storm.

125. The wax at his mouth cracked,

126. and a sound like the groaning of wood escaped.

127. And the priests fell upon their faces, crying:

128. "Lo, the Gospel speaks through silence broken! Write it! Write it quickly!"

129. And the scribes wrote:

130. The Gospel groaned as thunder, and heaven answered with stillness.

131. But Asael knew the sound was not thunder, nor was it stillness,

132. but the cry of a boy whose lips had forgotten how to part.

133. And in the days that followed his body began to tremble more fiercely.

134. The cords strained against his wrists and the pearls upon his robe cracked like teeth.

135. And the people cried:

136. "Behold the Gospel, wrestling with God!

137. See how holiness writhes within him!"

138. And the scribes wrote:

139. He trembled, and the pillars of the earth trembled with him.

140. He shook, and the mountains did bow.

141. But Asael whispered within his mind,

142. a voice no ink could hear:

143. It is not the mountains that bow, it is only my body, breaking.

144. And pilgrims brought knives wrapped in velvet saying:

145. "Touch them to his robe, and they will cut sin."

146. And others brought jars of honey, saying:

147. "Place them at his feet, and they will sweeten death."

148. And still others brought bowls of ash, saying:

303

149. "Scatter them by his breath and even cinders will be sanctified."

150. And Asael beheld these things, and thought, they hunger not for God, but for themselves.

151. They drink not of heaven, but of my marrow.

152. And his silence pressed upon him like a shroud.

153. Then the high priest rose before the multitude and lifted a scroll sealed with seven drops of wax.

154. And he cried aloud:

155. "This is the covenant of Asael, the Bound Gospel.

156. He shall remain forever in silence, that the silence may speak.

157. He shall remain forever in stillness, that the stillness may move us.

158. He shall remain forever bound, that the binding may set us free."

159. And all the people shouted, Amen.

160. And the scroll was opened,

161. and the words were laid upon the altar, beside Asael himself,

162. so that ink and flesh were bound together as twin testaments.

163. And in that hour Asael felt the cords not only upon his wrists, but upon his very name.

164. For when they spake it, it was no longer his own.

165. And he thought, if this be gospel then gospel is theft.

166. But he spoke not.

167. For his mouth was sealed.

168. And even his silence was no longer his own.

169. And thus it was declared throughout the land:

170. "There is no scripture save the Bound Gospel,

171. and the Bound Gospel is Asael,

172. and Asael is silence,

173. and silence is God."

174. And the multitude fell to their knees,

175. and their voices rose in praise,

176. but Asael's heart sank as into a pit,

177. for he beheld that he had been made into a book of scripture.

178. He had been made into a relic of blasphemy.

179. He had been made into a vessel for God.

180. And all the while, a boy still trembled beneath the cords.

181. And his trembling became their law,

182. and his silence their psalm,

183. and his sorrow their salvation.

Hymn IV

1. And it came to pass, after the binding, that Asael was lifted upon the altar as a lamp, yet gave no light.

2. By day he lay unmoving, his silence thicker than gold.

3. By night he trembled, and the cords about him creaked as branches in storm.

4. And the people said, Behold, the relic shakes with the breath of heaven.

5. And they wrote in their books: He who shakes does so for our sins.

6. Pilgrims gathered from far fields, bringing offerings of wheat, oil, and ash.

7. They pressed their foreheads to his feet, though the skin there had split from strain.

8. And they kissed the cords that bruised his wrists, saying, Lo, even the bruises are covenant.

9. Yet Asael wept within, though no sound passed his lips.

10. His tears rolled as glass beads upon his cheeks, and the priests gathered them in chalices, saying, Drink, for this is purity made water.

11. And the novices prayed beside his silence, reciting psalms until their voices cracked,

12. but he gave no answer, for the wax held firm, and the cords burned deeper.

13. And the people cried: Behold, silence itself has become a voice!

14. And they wrote: He who speaks not speaks loudest. He who answers not answers forever.

15. Then a mother brought her sick child and laid him at Asael's bound feet.

16. And she whispered, If thou art relic, heal him by thy silence.

17. And the child ceased weeping, for he fell into slumber.

18. And the people lifted their hands, saying, Lo, a miracle has bloomed!

19. Yet Asael knew: the child had only slept.

20. Still they named it miracle, and they wrote: He heals not with hand, but with quiet. He cures not with breath, but with stillness.

21. And thus his silence was chained to their hope,

22. and his body to their hunger.

23. In the watches of the night, Asael trembled harder, for the cords bit and the wax cracked.

24. His chest heaved as a bellows, but no flame arose.

25. And in his mind he cried out, Loosen me, O Lord, for I am no altar but flesh!

26. But the heavens gave no answer.

27. And the priests, hearing his bindings creak, fell prostrate, crying: The relic sings in silence! Blessed be the relic!

28. Then they clothed him in blue veils and said, Hide the boy, keep only the relic.

29. And they wrote upon the veils with golden thread: This is the silence of God, wrapped and preserved.

30. And Asael thought: They do not pray to me. They pray through me. And I am lost behind their prayers.

31. Thus the Relic of Silence was established.

32. And the multitude bowed, chanting: Holy, holy, holy is the silence of Asael.

33. And his trembling was lost in the roar of their praise.

34. Yet in his heart he vowed: This silence is not mine. And one day, it shall break.

35. And lo, the steward decreed: Every silence is to be counted, and every tremble recorded.

36. And the novices took quills, dipping them in ink, and watched him without ceasing.

37. They wrote: At the first hour, he shook as if lightning passed within.

38. They wrote: At the second hour, his lips glistened as dew upon the Ark.

39. They wrote: At the third hour, his eyelids fluttered, and behold, it was as the wings of cherubim.

40. And these records were bound in red leather, gilded at the spine,

41. and pilgrims kissed the books as they passed, saying, The relic has spoken in stillness, and it has been written.

42. Then the priests brought forth basins of oil,

43. and when Asael's silence deepened, they anointed his feet, whispering: Lo, silence anoints silence, as river anoints stone.

44. But the oil stung his sores, and the wounds swelled as flowers in summer heat.

45. Yet still they cried: The relic blooms! The relic bears fruit in pain!

46. And behold, a man blind from youth was led to the altar.

47. He touched the cords upon Asael's wrist, and when he turned away, he swore he saw shadows dance like light.

48. The multitude rejoiced, saying, The relic has opened his eyes!

49. But Asael looked upon him and saw the same white gaze, clouded and unseeing.

50. And Asael's heart trembled more than his body, for even falsehoods grew as faith.

51. Then the sisters, desiring fragments of blessing, gathered the wax that dripped from his sealed mouth.

52. They moulded candles of it, thin and pale, and lit them upon sickbeds.

53. And when any sleeper stirred, they cried, Lo, the relic's silence has passed into the flame!

54. And Asael thought: Every drop they gather is mine. Every silence they kindle devours me further.

55. But no word rose in him, for silence was now heavier than sound.

56. And it was decreed that none should touch him save with veils and gloves.

57. For the priests said: He is too holy to be handled as flesh. He is vessel, not boy.

58. And thus his warmth grew strange to him, for none touched him as skin.

59. In the watches of the night, he felt his body ache as though pressed into stone.

60. He thought: I am becoming reliquary.

61. He thought: My marrow has been traded for glass.

62. And though his mind screamed, the cords smothered the sound, and the people heard only silence.

63. And they rejoiced, saying: The relic is content, for silence is perfection.

64. Then came a day when a youth dared press his ear close to Asael's chest.

65. He heard the thrum of blood and whispered, The relic sings beneath the silence.

66. And the priests declared: Every beat of his heart is a hymn, though unheard by the common ear.

67. And the youth was beaten for presuming to listen too closely.

68. And Asael wept within, for the boy was nearer to truth than all their prayers.

69. And the multitude, increasing, crowded the chapel until air itself grew thin.

70. And every pilgrim carried silence as an offering: mouths closed, eyes lowered, steps measured.

71. And they whispered: We bring our silence to feed his silence. May silence multiply silence forevermore.

72. Thus silence became his prison, wrapped in veils, fed by worship, chained by praise.

73. And Asael thought: I am not silence. I am voice withheld.

74. Yet none heard him, for the cords cut deeper, and wax sealed every trembling word.

75. And the people rejoiced still, saying: The relic's silence is eternal.

Hymn V

1. And it came to pass in those days that Asael was set upon the altar, bound in cords white and gold.

2. His mouth was sealed with wax, his hands with silk, his eyes lowered to stone.

3. And the multitude gathered, pilgrims from near and far, filling the chapel with breath held as incense.

4. And the priests declared: Behold, the Living Gospel! Behold, the Silent Word!

5. And the people brought offerings of salt and honey, of feathers gathered from fields, of children laid at his feet.

6. And they said: We pray not to him, but through him, for silence makes way for the divine.

7. And they lit candles of his wax, and the smoke rose as a pillar, and they sang hymns without voice, only mouths moving.

8. And Asael trembled upon the altar.

9. The cords bit deeper, as vines upon a tree.

10. The wax upon his lips cracked, but still no sound was loosed.

11. And the people rejoiced, saying: The relic shakes with ecstasy, the relic quivers with the nearness of God.

12. And the priests set him higher, raising the altar upon steps of marble, so that all might gaze upon his stillness.

13. And they placed a crown of woven reeds upon his brow, dipped in oil until it gleamed as gold.

14. And the reeds cut into his skin, bleeding slow rivers down his cheeks.

15. And the sisters gathered the blood in basins, whispering, every drop is blessing.

16. And lo, the reliquary was opened, and Asael was set within as one sets bread within a vessel.

17. And the doors were glass, and the hinges sealed, so that all could see and none could touch.

18. And the multitude pressed lips to the glass, whispering prayers, leaving marks of breath as offerings.

19. Asael's body shook, not in reverence but in suffocation.

20. And his mind thundered: I am not silence. I am voice withheld.

21. Yet the cords held, and the wax burned his lips, and his throat seared with unshed sound.

22. And one among the novices cried out: Look! The relic weeps!

23. For tears streamed from Asael's eyes, though bitter as brine and hot as fire.

24. And the priests proclaimed: The relic weeps for our sins. The relic weeps the tears of God.

25. And the multitude fell upon their knees, and their silence deepened, and their devotion became as chains heavier than iron.

26. And Asael's heart beat like a drum, but each beat was swallowed by their worship.

27. He though, if I cry, I will shatter them. If I do not, I will be devoured.

28. And he dreamed while waking that his ribs split like doors, and inside them bloomed a furnace.

29. The furnace groaned, the fire pressed against his skin, and still no sound escaped.

30. Until at last the fire kissed his throat, whispering: Speak, or burn forever silent.

31. And Asael opened his mouth beneath the wax, and the wax cracked as clay, and blood welled, and fire surged.

32. And in the stillness of a thousand kneeling souls, the cords trembled as if they knew what was to come.

33. And all heaven and earth

leaned close.

34. And the multitude pressed closer, their knees grinding into the stone, their palms outstretched as if the air around him were holy to touch.

35. And though Asael's breath came in gasps, they called it rhythm, they called it prayer.

36. And though his skin flushed with fever, they called it radiance, they called it light.

37. A woman laid her child at the base of the altar, whispering: Breathe, and be blessed.

38. And when the child stirred, kicking once in sleep, they proclaimed: Lo, the relic has given life!

39. And the story spread through the nave like fire, each pilgrim swearing they had seen the babe rise by Asael's trembling alone.

40. And the priests lifted their hands, commanding silence, though silence already smothered the air.

41. And one cried: The relic speaks without words!

42. And another: The relic heals

without touch!

43. And the multitude echoed their words as scripture, though Asael wept, though he bled, though he burned unseen.

44. And lo, a man touched the glass and swore he felt heat upon his fingers.

45. And another swore he saw wings unfurl, though Asael was bound.

46. And another swore he heard a hymn sung low, though Asael's lips were sealed in wax.

47. And the priests proclaimed: Every vision is true, for the relic bends the world into miracles.

48. And Asael's body quaked, not with vision but with horror, for every lie chained him tighter than cords.

49. He thought: I am drowning beneath their belief. Their faith is the water that fills my lungs.

50. Yet still the multitude rejoiced, chanting his name as if it were no longer his but theirs.

51. And they called: Asael, Asael, Asael, until the name lost shape, until it rang as hollow as bells

313

cracked by fire.

52. And Asael heard not his name, but the echo of an empty vessel.

53. He thought: They do not pray to me. They pray through me. And through me, I am gone.

54. And a novice, trembling, approached the altar with a vial of oil.

55. She dripped the oil upon the cords, and it seeped into Asael's skin, stinging like fire.

56. She whispered: Anointing is not pain, anointing is purity.

57. And though Asael bit his tongue until blood filled his mouth, they called it blessing.

58. And behold, the reliquary glass began to fog from his heat.

59. And they declared: The relic breathes holiness, and the air itself bows to him.

60. Yet Asael knew it was only the furnace of his body, only the fire sealed within.

61. And still, he could not speak.

62. Then the steward brought forth a book, gilt-edged and empty of ink.

63. He held it high and cried: Every word the relic utters in silence shall be written here, for silence is greater than speech.

64. And though no word came, they filled the book with testimonies, each pilgrim swearing they had heard what was never said.

65. And Asael's vision swam.

66. His throat seared as if with molten lead, pressing against the seal.

67. He thought: If I do not cry out, I shall burst and stain this place with what they cannot sanctify.

68. Yet still he held, for the cords were strong, and the fear stronger.

69. And all the while the multitude sang his silence, and the chapel walls trembled as if the stones themselves were weary of their worship.

70. And the wax upon his lips cracked again, faint as thunder far away.

71. And the priests fell prostrate,

crying: The relic prepares a great miracle. Wait, wait, wait upon the silence of God.

72. And lo, the multitude rose as one, their voices clashing, each proclaiming visions greater than the last.

73. One cried: I saw the relic crowned with flame.

74. Another: I heard the relic sing the lost name of God.

75. And still another: I felt my sins lift from me as dust in wind when I touched the glass.

76. And the priests lifted their hands, but they could not still the flood of voices.

77. And it was written: When belief grows louder than God, it becomes its own scripture.

78. And Asael quivered, for each word bound him deeper, each vision another nail in flesh not yet dead.

79. And the cords about his wrists strained, cutting lines into his skin.

80. His veins pulsed with fire; his breath boiled against the wax.

81. He thought: I am not vessel, I am not gospel. I am only a boy suffocating before an altar.

82. And the wax cracked again, a thin fissure gleaming red with blood.

83. And the crowd roared, crying: The relic bleeds for us! The relic prepares the covenant!

84. And their joy struck Asael like hammers, for they saw only miracle where there was only wound.

85. Then a storm rose without, lashing rain against the chapel stones.

86. And they proclaimed: The heavens themselves bow to the relic's silence.

87. But Asael knew the storm was within, a tempest clawing at his chest, begging release.

88. And a child pressed close to the reliquary, eyes wide as moons.

89. She whispered: Relic, tell me the name of my mother who forgot me.

90. And Asael wept, for he knew if he spoke, the child would

forget not only her mother but her own face.

91. Yet they cried: See, the relic weeps in mercy!

92. And lo, a novice fainted at his feet, crying she had seen angels swarming behind his shoulders.

93. And another tore his robe, swearing feathers fell upon him like snow.

94. And they gathered the torn cloth, the imagined feathers, and built an altar within an altar, a shrine within a shrine.

95. And Asael felt the marrow of his bones soften, his body trembling as though already dissolving.

96. And he thought: They are not waiting for me to cry. They are waiting for me to break.

97. And the wax pulsed now with each heartbeat, a seal of flesh ready to burst.

98. And the priests lifted incense, smoke choking the chamber until the air itself grew thick.

99. And Asael inhaled, and the smoke curled into his throat like thorns.

100. He felt it coil with the feathers within, heavy, pressing upward.

101. And he thought: When I break, I will tear heaven itself open.

102. And the multitude, wild with frenzy, struck their chests and wailed.

103. Some clawed their eyes until blood ran, crying: We will not see until the relic speaks.

104. Others rent their tongues, crying: We will not speak until the relic cries out.

105. And the chapel trembled with their fervour.

106. And Asael's silence was now thunder, each breath rattling stone.

107. The reliquary shook; the cords split like veins beneath a blade.

108. And the priests fell prostrate, declaring: The great utterance is near. The relic will cry, and the world shall be remade.

109. And Asael, choking, burning, breaking, thought one last thought: If I open, I will end them. If I stay closed, I will end myself.

110. And the choice was torn from him, for the wax cracked in full, bursting wide.

111. And silence itself shattered.

112. And the wax burst from his lips like oil from a lamp.

113. The cords snapped as if they had always been threads of smoke.

114. And the reliquary trembled as a heart trembles before death.

115. And Asael opened his mouth.

116. And no word came forth.

117. Only a sound older than language, sharper than thunder, softer than mourning.

118. And the sound moved through the chapel like a living thing.

119. It passed through flesh as wind through reeds.

120. It entered bone and hollowed it like a flute.

121. And the pilgrims who knelt fell sideways as stalks in a gale.

122. Some forgot their own names.

123. Some forgot their dead.

124. Some forgot their hands, staring as if at strangers' fingers.

125. And the priests tried to pray but the prayers dissolved on their tongues.

126. And the windows burst outward, glass flying as birds released.

127. And the painted saints blurred, their eyes turning blank, their swords and lilies vanishing.

128. And Asael cried again, and the stone beneath him cracked, splitting like dry bread.

129. And the reliquary shook itself apart, gold filigree curling into dust.

130. And the altar lifted from the floor as though borne on an unseen tide.

131. And the sound rose higher still, until the roof lifted and the sky came pouring in.

132. And the clouds tore open like veils.

133. And the heavens themselves

bent low, listening.

134. And the world outside shook; mountains cracked; rivers reversed their course; bells rang without hands.

135. And creatures of the field knelt with faces to the earth, though no one had called them.

136. And every mirror shattered, sending back not faces but wings.

137. And Asael stood in the centre of the ruin, mouth open, soundless now, but the echo still roaring, a pillar of noise climbing into the dark.

138. And the people covered their ears, their eyes, their mouths, but there was no refuge.

139. For this was not a sound. This was the unmaking of silence.

140. And lo, the last cords fell from his wrists.

141. And the wax dripped from his chin like molten stars.

142. And his feathers burned and did not burn, light pouring from them like spilled dawn.

143. And they cried, The relic lives!

144. And they cried, The relic dies!

145. And they cried, The relic is God!

146. But Asael spoke at last, his words a sacrament:

147. "I am not your prayer."

148. And the word split the chapel down the middle.

149. And the walls fell outward.

150. And the roof rose upward.

151. And the floor sank like a ship into the earth.

152. And the people fell as shadows fall.

153. And the sky poured in like a flood of white fire.

154. And the voice went out into the world, and the world cracked like clay.

155. And behold, the Rapture.

156. Not of lifting, but a breaking.

157. Not of silence, but a sound without end.

158. And Asael, mouth open,

stood alone in the ruin of the altar.

159. And the people fled or vanished or were lifted, none could say which.

160. And the last thing he saw was not the chapel, but the sky itself, trembling as if it had a heartbeat.

161. And thus was written the end of the Bound Gospel.

162. And thus began the Cry.

163. And there was no Amen.

The Lozère Times Issue No. 405 | February 9th, 1999 Front Page, Faith & Society

"The Sleeping Saint of Lozère"

Whispers of a Miracle at St. Luden's Chapel

By Claudette Hale, Staff Correspondent

LOZÈRE, FRANCE

Tucked behind a wall of ancient ivy and thin mist, the rural chapel of St. Luden's has, until recently, stood quiet as the grave. But in recent weeks, something—someone—has brought hushed pilgrimage and curious reverence to its pews.

That someone is known only as J.M., a young man described by visiting clergy as "a vessel touched by grace." The Church has not publicly named him, nor spoken on how he came to reside in the old chapel. But within Lozère and its surrounding parishes, the story travels in snippets: a brilliant but strange boy; a journal written in symbols and scripture; a voice that spoke softly, but never to anyone in the room.

Now, he does not speak at all.

"He's beautiful," said one nun, requesting anonymity. "Like a statue made of breath. You feel something in your bones when you see him. Not fear. Not exactly. But something very close to grief."

Descriptions vary, but consistent details have emerged: pale skin like polished marble, hair combed carefully down the back in waves, limbs wrapped gently in linen, posture always perfect—sometimes seated, sometimes standing in a shaft of chapel light. His hands remain gloved. His mouth is never visible beneath a soft cloth veil, rumoured to be laced with myrrh and crushed rose.

Though visitors are rarely permitted, those who have been granted access speak of the experience in devotional tones.

"He doesn't move. He doesn't blink. But you know he's aware," said Father Ellory, a deacon from nearby Drôme. "There's no suffering in him. Only stillness. It feels holy."

Parishioners have begun calling him The Sleeping Saint.

No miracles have been formally attributed to his presence, though a child with night terrors reportedly slept soundly after placing a feather beneath his pillow. A farmer's wife claims to have conceived after laying her rosary on the chapel's threshold. Others simply leave notes and flowers.

Yet not all are convinced.

"I've seen things like this before," said Dr. Hannah Ley, a scholar of ritual pathology. "Spiritualized suffering. The Church has a long history of making relics out of the vulnerable. We should be asking where his family is. What he consented to. If anything."

Still, St. Luden's has not responded to requests for comment.

Behind its doors, the boy remains—silent, motionless, lit by waxlight. Some say he is praying. Others say he is listening. But one thing is agreed upon by all who have seen him:

He is watching.

And he weeps.

Postscript I

Filed by Callum Ward, Junior Editor & Assistant Archivist

Project: *Feather Tongue*, **J.M. Errevale**

Filed From: Hillsather House

Date: [REDACTED]

I don't know how to do this properly. There's a format I'm supposed to follow—introductory notes, provenance, editorial context. I've used it before. But it feels wrong here. Too clean. Too distant.

So... I guess I'll start at the beginning.

The tapes arrived in a battered cardboard box, unmarked except for a single word scrawled on the top: "Listen." No return address. No sender. Only the weight of something that someone needed to be found. Nothing new for Hillsather, we've received manuscripts in stranger ways.

The tapes were numbered in fading ink, many of them damaged, spliced, or partially overwritten. Alongside them was a thin manuscript—handwritten, most pages smudged, a few near illegible.

We knew the name J.M. Errevale, I guess in the way someone knows the name of a saint you've never prayed to.

Once whispered.

Once published.

Then gone.

Originally, it was supposed to be on Mr. Lowre's desk, he's usually the one handling completed manuscripts. But he offered it to me. Said Errevale needed someone that felt the weight as clearly as he did.

I didn't know what he meant by it then, so naturally, I accepted. A senior editor offering a junior such a big piece? I jumped on it.

And now I'm thinking I shouldn't have. I wasn't ready. But I think maybe no one ever is.

As I listened, and read, and listened again, I found myself speaking to the pages. Whispering things like *I'm sorry* or *I hear you.* I told myself it was part of the process. But the truth is, I started to feel like I wasn't reading Errevale—he was speaking to me. And whatever he said, he wanted me to write it down.

I don't want to frame this as a tragedy. It is one, of course. But it's more than that. It's a document of someone trying so desperately to be known, to be held, to be understood in a language that no one around him seemed willing to learn.

That language, it turns out, was made of feathers and blood and cassette tape.

Callum Ward

More in Postscript II: Visitation

Postscript II: Visitation

Filed by Callum Ward, Junior Editor & Assistant Archivist
Location: St. Luden's Chapel, Lozère (formerly Redacted)
Filed Date: [CLASSIFIED]

I arrived just after dawn. The chapel was already condemned, boarded, padlocked, and posted with enough "DO NOT ENTER" signage to make even the bravest researcher pause.

I paused for about six seconds.

Technically, I have clearance. Hillsather has a way of opening doors. But this wasn't about official permission—it was about Errevale. About standing in the place where he whispered into a recorder and prayed into silence. I didn't come just to document it. I came to feel it.

The chapel had been shut down less than a year prior, after a string of police investigations prompted by anonymous reports— some credible, others hysterical. Allegations of ritualistic abuse, unexplained injuries, unexplained disappearances. Officially, nothing was confirmed. Unofficially, a nun was hospitalized for nerve damage in both hands, and a young boy went missing. He was never found.

The Church denied everything. Said the records were falsified. Said the chapel had simply "fallen into disrepair."

It smelled like more than that.

Inside, mold climbed the walls like ivy. Glass shattered inward instead of out. Candles burnt to the base and left, as if someone expected them to relight.

It smelled… strange. Not just of dust and disuse. There was something beneath it. Iron. Wax. Something vaguely sweet and sickening, like old fruit left behind by something that could not eat it.

I took notes for the first half hour, walking the nave and snapping photos. But then I found the first sealed room. The dormitory.

It had a cross nailed through the handle and a paper warning pinned to the door—"Do Not Disturb Until Closure."

So naturally, I disturbed it.

The lock was laughable. And honestly, if they didn't want people going in, they should have tried harder. I slipped inside and closed the door behind me, breathing in stale air and an unmistakable chill. The beds were stripped, but faint outlines remained on the sheets where people had once lain. There was a box of old cassette players beneath one of the bunks. Dusty. Untouched.

I sat down on the bed with the least amount of dust and just took it all in.

There was nothing magical. No great revelation. But something settled in me then, something I still don't have words for. Like grief finding a shape. Like the air was waiting for someone to come back.

I moved on. The chapel itself—the actual altar room—was sealed tighter, with crime scene tape and remnants of salt still lining the threshold. I didn't cross that one. I don't know why. Maybe because it felt like crossing into a wound. If Lowre tells me to come back for it, I will. But not now.

I did, however, find his room. The one from the tapes. It had no label. Just a brass doorknob and a splintered threshold.

Inside, everything was wrong. Not ruined—just wrong. The walls were peeling in long, curling scrolls, the window was nailed shut from the outside, and the ceiling had a patch that looked like someone had tried to scrub blood from it and given up halfway through. There was a desk with a broken drawer and a feather pressed into the spine of a hymnal.

I took the feather. I know I shouldn't have. But I had to.

It wasn't about theft. It was more… communion.

I sat at the desk and played one of the tapes again. Cassette 001. He sounds so young in that one. Hopeful. Tired. Trying so hard to explain something no one else would believe.

I didn't cry, exactly. But I pressed my forehead to the desk and let myself sit in it—in all of it. The silence. The echo. The ache.

When I finally left, I pinned a chair under the knob to seal the room behind me again. Someone should, I think.

Not to hide it.

But to protect what's still echoing there.

He deserved a locked room again.

I've sent the recordings and notes back to Hillsather for archival. But this entry is personal. I'll file it if I must. But I don't think it belongs in a drawer.

It belongs with the story. With him. J.M. Errevale.

Wherever he is.

C. Ward

The Lozère Times Issue No. 452 | August 17th, 2006 Front Page, Faith & Investigation

"The Saint Who Wasn't"

St. Luden's Chapel Shuttered Amid Scandal, Corpse Discovered in Altar Display

By Claudette Hale, Senior Correspondent

LOZÈRE, FRANCE

Years after glowing headlines declared a "miracle" at St. Luden's Anglican Chapel, a grim truth has surfaced; the so-called Sleeping Saint of Lozère was, in fact, a well-preserved corpse—dressed, posed, and displayed before a congregation of faithful believers.

Authorities confirmed the body's discovery last week following an anonymous report citing "unbearable odour" and "suspicion of neglect." What investigators found was far worse: an adolescent male, deceased for an estimated five to six months, arranged in ceremonial attire and veiled from the neck down. He was positioned upright—his posture supported internally with reinforced wire and hidden scaffolding.

Despite early speculation, the cause of death is listed as exsanguination due to cranial trauma, with post-mortem evidence of extensive ritual handling, including superficial carvings along the spine, scalp, and arms. Feathers—many stitched directly into the skin—had begun to yellow. The scent of decay had been masked by layers of incense, clove oil, and rosewater.

The boy was identified through partial dental records as James Michael Errevale, a reclusive youth believed to have lived at the chapel since childhood. His family remains untraceable.

No charges have yet been filed, but authorities are investigating several former clergy members and laypersons affiliated with St. Luden's final years of operation. At least two nuns and a former deacon remain unaccounted for.

Locals are divided.

"I believed he was blessed," said one parishioner, who had once left a rosary near the chapel door. "They said he spoke to angels. That he glowed under candlelight. I never imagined he was—dead."

Others are less surprised.

"That chapel always gave me the chills," muttered the owner of a local grocer. "Too quiet. Too clean. And that smell... always like flowers gone to rot."

In retrospect, several visitors had raised concerns that were ignored or dismissed. One pilgrim wrote anonymously that the boy "didn't blink or breathe," and another claimed "his mouth never moved—even when he 'spoke.'" These warnings were never formally investigated until the odour became too severe to conceal.

The Diocese of Exeter released a brief statement:

"We are deeply saddened by the tragedy at St. Luden's and remain committed to assisting authorities in their inquiry. The individual known as 'J.M.' was under private clerical care due to extraordinary medical needs. The recent findings were unknown to the Diocese at large. We offer our prayers for all involved."

But questions remain, how long had the chapel's staff known?

Who orchestrated the rituals?

And why did no one step forward sooner? For now, the chapel has been declared a crime scene. The altar has been sealed, and no further access is permitted.

Outside the gates, pilgrims continue to arrive—some weeping, others burning candles, still others clawing the soil for feathers.

A new phrase has begun to appear in chalk across nearby roads and benches:

"He weeps still."

Postscript III

I keep thinking about how young he was.

Nineteen.

I've read that number a hundred times now, typed it in summaries, signed it in reports.

But it never stays just a number.

It's a face. A boy. A voice in a cassette saying goodnight to no one.

He was nineteen when they took him from himself. Nineteen when they cut the feathers to fit, when they bottled his blood and passed it around like relic water. Nineteen, and the world swallowed him whole.

I was nineteen when I lost my faith. Not violently. Just… quietly. It just kinda slipped off me. Like an old shirt that didn't fit anymore. No lightning. No great betrayal. Just a growing silence that I didn't know how to pray through.

Sometimes I wonder… if we'd crossed paths at the right time, in the right chapel, in some flickering hallway between two aching childhoods—Would we have known each other? We're close in age, would I have been like a big brother to him?

I think he would've smiled softly. Said little. Maybe called me a pilgrim.

And I, idiot that I am, would've asked what it was like to hear God's voice.

He would've laughed at that. Maybe not out loud. But in his eyes.

It's absurd, I know. To imagine friendship in the margins of posthumous manuscript. But after months listening to his voice— his real voice, cracking and wondering and trying so hard not to cry—I can't pretend he was just a subject. Or a saint. Or a file on my desk.

He was a boy. He was scared. And he never got to choose what kind of miracle he became.

So I did something stupid.

I used half a month's pay—probably more than I should've—and bought him a gravestone. A small one. Limestone. Simple.

It doesn't have his name. Just a date.

I had it placed in a little plot in Wiltshire. There's sun there. Trees. Space. It's open and quiet, and no one expects anything of the dead there. No prayers. No worship. Just rest.

I know his body isn't there. God, I wish it was.

But maybe… maybe this way he can still have something. A place. A birthday. A place to age, if only in spirit. A place to wait for no one.

Maybe now, at last, he can spend the rest of his birthdays outside.

Alone.

And in warm silence.
C. Ward

ADDITIONS

I debated for a long time whether to include these last recordings.

They were never meant for the public—at least, not the way the others were. They lack the structure, the ritual cadence, that strange grace that made the earlier tapes so easy for the chapel to canonize. These ones are smaller, quieter. You can hear him laughing sometimes. You can hear him ask questions no one ever answered.

Some part of me thought I'd be doing him a disservice by adding them. He deserves something that's just for him.

But I kept coming back to them.

Because I think they matter more than any sermon ever could.

The world was too eager to turn J.M. Errevale into something divine. To twist his words and press them flat until they looked like prophecy. But what I hear in these tapes isn't divinity. It's just… curiosity. It's fear. It's a boy trying to understand the shape of his own voice before everyone else decided what it meant.

He talks about stories he wanted to write. About birds nesting in the chapel roof. About how ink smells when it's fresh and dark enough to swallow the light. He wonders what the world looks like beyond the cloister walls, if the wind sounds different in the open. He questions his upbringing, questions himself.

He wonders who he would have been, if they'd let him live long enough to find out.

I can't give him that, but I can give him this. A chance to be remembered whole.

Not as a vessel.

Not as a saint.

But as a boy who was curious, and lonely, and brave enough to keep recording even when no one was listening.

So I've placed these final cassettes here, at the end.

Not as evidence of his boyhood.

Just as evidence that he lived.

Callum Ward

ERREVALE

CASSETTE A

[Click.]

[Soft ambient noise, perhaps the gentle creak of his bed as he adjusts the recorder close to his mouth. There's hesitation in his breath.]

I think I'm alone.

[A long pause. A swallow.]

I waited until the lamps were out and the bells stopped. Everyone's supposed to be asleep by now. Even the sisters.

[He whispers, conspiratorial.]

I just want to try something.

[Another pause. Then—quietly, like he's afraid the walls will tell on him.]

Fuck.

[Silence. Then—he gasps.]

Oh—

[A shaky breath. Then a soft, disbelieving laugh.]

I said it.

No one struck me down.
The ceiling didn't crack. Nothing caught fire.

[He whispers again, urgent now.]

I said it.

[Another long pause. The thrill and the horror catch in his throat.]

I read it once—in a novel Sister Hesper let me borrow by mistake. She didn't get to that page. I don't think she would've given it to me if she had.

I wrote the word down and hid it behind my mattress. I've looked at it for weeks. Every night. Like it's some kind of spell.

And tonight I said it.

[He laughs again, breathlessly. Then quieter.]

I don't know if that means I'm bad now.
I don't feel bad.
I feel… here.
Like the word put something back inside me.
Like I'm not just the story they're writing.

[A beat. He lowers his voice, near a whisper.]

Maybe saints aren't supposed to swear.
Or want.
But I want… something.
I don't even know what.
Just something more.

[He exhales slowly, then with a barely audible smile in his voice;]

Maybe that's sin.

Maybe sin is wanting.

And maybe that's not the worst thing after all.

[A pause. Then, cheekily, under his breath;]

Fuck.

[He laughs again—quiet, boyish, and golden. Then silence. He speaks once more, soft and almost bashful.]

Goodnight.

[Click.]

CASSETTE B

[Click.]

[A soft exhale. The microphone picks up faint rustling, like linen sheets shifting. A clock chimes distantly—three bells. Errevale speaks slowly, sleepily.]

I had a dream last night.

Not a vision. Not a holy whisper. Just… a dream.

There was someone in it. I couldn't see their face. Only their hands. They touched my hair and said my name like they knew it wasn't meant to be prayed to.

Just… spoken.

[He pauses, then laughs under his breath.]

That doesn't sound like much, does it? But it felt more sacred than anything the priests ever say.

Because it was for me. Not the saint. Not a prophet. Just… me.

[He shifts, fabric rustling. Then a long breath.]

I wonder what it's like to be loved.

I don't mean the hymns. Or the scriptures. I mean—real love.

The kind that doesn't require miracles.

The kind that lets you mess up. That lets you fall asleep with your mouth open and still get kissed in the morning.

[A pause. He speaks lower now.]

There's a novice, I won't say who, but when she laughs, she forgets to bow.

And when she says my name, she says it like it's still a boy's name.

Not a title. Not a relic.

Just Errevale.

I think... I think I have a crush on her.

[He laughs softly. Then covers it with a hand—you can hear the brush of fingers over the mic.]

It's not allowed, of course.

They say love must be given to God first. That everything else is lesser. But what if God made love so we could learn how to choose it?

What if the holiest thing I ever do is hold someone's hand?

[He pauses. Then speaks slower, dreamier.]

That sounds silly, doesn't it? But how nice it must be, to hold a hand without reverence. Or even just... the reverence of care, and not sanctity.

[He pauses, then hums to himself quietly.]

[Click.]

CASSETTE C

[Click.]

[A faint scrape of wood, maybe a chair being dragged. The rustle of parchment, the soft scratch of a quill. Errevale sighs—dramatic, thoughtful.]

Is it a sin to want to know?

I'm not talking about heresy. Not... exactly. I mean little things. Things I've never asked out loud. Like—why is it wrong to say fuck?

[He gasps softly, then laughs—part shocked, part delighted.]

I said it.

I did.

And nothing happened. No lightning. No angels tearing open the roof.

It just... sat there.

[A pause. He exhales again. His voice lowers.]

I read a passage this morning in Leviticus. Something about garments of mixed fabrics. About how even thread can offend heaven.

But then I think of Sister Amica's quilt, and how it's stitched with every colour she could find, and how she lets the orphans curl up in it when they're sick—and how could that be sinful?

How could warmth be wicked?

[He scoffs under his breath—uncertain if it's safe to laugh.]

And then there's the other parts. The parts they never read aloud.

[He clears his throat, bashfully.]

The ones about men and men. Women and women. The parts that get whispered over in chapel, like the syllables themselves might stain the altar.

But if love is patient, and love is kind... How is it wrong?

[A rustle—he's moving closer to the mic, voice quieter now.]

I saw two boys kiss once. Years ago, in the back of the chapel garden. I wasn't skipping vespers. Not really. I was just... taking my time. And I saw them, hushing each other's laughs. I remember because one of them had a scar under his eye, and he closed it when they kissed. Like he was praying.

And I didn't feel disgusted.

I felt… envious.

Not of them, I don't think. Just of what they had.

The right to kiss someone and not be turned into a parable. But I suppose their lives are a sort of parable, isn't it? The kind that's chastised. Father Bell says God destroyed a city for such things but… we're still here. Lozère has yet to be struck down.

[A pause. He laughs softly—unsettled, but sincere.]

Is that the sin?

Wanting without permission?

[Then, with mock gravity, like reading a royal edict;]

Thou shalt not want, lest you make the story about yourself.

[He clears his throat. The next words come in a rush.]

I said fuck again just a bit ago. There—I did it twice.

Maybe three times if I say it again.

…Fuck.

[A beat. Then, gleeful and horrified;]

Oh no. I'm doomed.

I'm going to be smote. Smited? Smoted? What's the past tense of divine wrath?

[He chuckles to himself—giddy, breathless.]

Maybe God has a sense of humour.

Maybe He's watching this recording right now, covering His face and thinking, "Why did I make this one so loud?"

[His voice softens. Reflective now.]

I don't want to be bad. I just want to know if I'm allowed to be curious. To want things. To say things. To laugh without wondering if it echoes wrong.

They say purity is a gift.

But I think curiosity is the better one.

[A pause. Then, mischievous again, whispered like a scandalous prayer;]

Amen, amen, and… fuck.

[Click.]

Cassette D

[Click.]

[The soft crackle of candlelight. Errevale's breath is calm at first. He speaks slowly, his voice older than before, touched with a brittle patience.]

They won't say the word. Not even when they lock the door behind me. Or when they touch my skin only with cloth.

Not even when I ask clearly, plainly, if I'll ever be allowed to leave.

They smile. They say, "You're safe here."

But they never say why I'm not allowed outside.

They never say what would happen if I was.

[A long pause. Then a faint laugh, not unkind—just hollow.]

The funny thing is, I don't think I want to run away.

Not really.

I just want someone to tell me what it means to stay.

[He shifts; you hear the soft clink of a rosary bead against his fingers.]

Today during morning study, I read the part in the Book of Matthew where Jesus says to "pluck out thine eye" if it causes sin.

I looked at the sisters after. And I thought, why haven't they done it? If they love God that much, why do they still have all their eyes?

[He laughs again—shorter this time, sharper. He regrets it.]

That's not fair.
I know that's not fair.
But sometimes I think holiness isn't about fairness at all.
It's about who survives the rules, and who becomes the rule itself.

[A long silence. Then he sighs.]

[Click.]

CASSETTE E

[Click.]

[Faint static, low and distant, like a chapel echo. The tone is soft, uncertain. Errevale's voice carries the stillness of someone newly unsettled.]

They watch me when I eat now.

Not all at once, not like a crowd or anything.

But I can feel them—just behind the thresholds.

The edge of the refectory, the lip of the choir screen.

Like I'm a flame they're afraid to smother...

but more afraid to leave alone.

[A pause. A swallow. Fabric shifts—he's likely seated.]

Sister Meryl dropped her spoon at supper tonight.

It clattered loud enough to break the prayer.

And everyone looked at her, horrified. Like she'd shattered something holy.

Like the silence belonged to me.

But I wasn't praying.

I was counting how many people bowed their heads before I did.

They take notes now.

Little books with ribbon markers.

One of them—Brother Caldus—I caught copying down something I said during breakfast.

Something stupid about the way the morning fog looked like milk poured over the hedgerow.

He wrote it down like scripture.

Like it meant something.

[He laughs softly, uncertain whether to find it funny or horrifying.]

Do you know what that feels like?

To become a collection of sentences?

To have your words stitched into linen and sung back to you?

They've started calling it The Errevale Doctrine.

Only whispers. Only among the senior clergy.

But I heard it. I heard them.

They think I don't know.

I caught my reflection in the reliquary glass.
It looked like I was behind it.

Like a relic.

My face… didn't move at first.
I had to blink to remind myself it was mine.

And for one terrifying second, I wondered if they'd replaced me with a more obedient version.

[He shifts. Something wooden creaks—perhaps the recorder on the table.]

I used to sing hymns with the others.
Now they hush when I enter.

They bow.

They light candles.

But no one sings.

No one sings around me anymore.

They think it's reverence.

But it feels like grief.

[His voice dips, softer now. Almost whispered, afraid someone might hear.]

I don't think I'm a boy to them anymore.

I'm a vessel. A symbol.

A moving picture they're too afraid to let fall out of frame.

And maybe the worst part is... part of me wants to give in.

To be perfect still. To be worshipped.

Because maybe then, they'll stop watching.

[A pause. His voice cracks just slightly.]

But if no one's watching...

do I still exist?

[He whispers now silently.]

Dear God, please... I don't want to be known.

I want to be seen.

Not studied.

Not remembered.

Just... seen.

[Click.]

CASSETTE F

[Click .]

[The sound of breathing, uneven. A chair creaks. Errevale's voice begins low, hesitant, but not afraid.]

I turned eighteen today, yet no one will tell me what it means.

Not truly.

The Bible says things like "a man shall not lie with a man as with a woman,"

but it never says why.

It talks about lust, about sin. About marriage as something that… redeems it.

Makes the ache acceptable.

But no one will tell me what the ache actually is.

No one will say the words.

[A pause. He shifts, and the faint sound of fingertips brushing cloth— maybe nervously, maybe absent-mindedly.]

I dreamt of Sister Loretta last week.

Not in a holy way.

She bent to light the altar candles and I saw the slope of her neck, the way the fabric of her dress pressed into her waist.

And I... I don't even know what it was, exactly.

Just heat.

My body reacting to something beautiful

in a way I couldn't control.

And then two days later, the courier boy came with the winter crates.

I didn't know his name. He had dirt on his knuckles and a cut lip. He smiled at me and called me sir.

Not vessel or blessed.

Just sir.

And I couldn't stop thinking about what his hands might feel like.

Rough. Warm. Real.

[He inhales sharply through his nose, clearly embarrassed. Then mutters;]

I shouldn't be saying this.

[A beat of quiet.]

But I have to say this somewhere.

Because no one will say it to me.

Not the nuns. Not Father Bell. Not the books.

They tell me what not to do. But never what to do with the feeling. Never why I feel this way.

Why I wake up aching.

Why I want to be touched.

Why something in me burns when I'm alone too long.

[A long hesitant silence. Then a whisper, guilt-frayed and trembling.]

I touched myself last night.

Not in the way they mean in sermons.

Not in defiance.

I didn't even mean to.

I just… felt the ache again.

The one that sits low in the belly like a fever trying to climb out.

And I pressed my hand… there…

Slow… soft… and something sparked.

It felt good.

Then better.

Then too much.

Like… the devil in the garden holding out an apple.

And when it ended… I cried.

[Another pause. He sounds smaller now. Uncertain.]

I don't know what I did.

I don't know if I'll go to Hell for it.

I don't know if I want to do it again or never again or only if someone else is watching to tell me I'm not damned.

[He laughs suddenly in bewilderment.]

God made this body.

He gave it hunger and breath and blood and touch.

And then called it wicked when I noticed how it felt.

How does that make sense?

Why give me this fire if all I'm allowed to do is smother it?

[A long silence. Then;]

Sometimes I think my body is a question and everyone here is too afraid to answer it.

So they pretend I'm not asking.

They pretend I'm not becoming.

But I am.

I *am.*

And if no one will teach me what it means to live in this skin,

then I'll have to learn it myself.

[His voice trembles now, torn between shame and defiance.]

I want someone to tell me I'm not unholy for wanting a mouth on my throat or wanting hands in the dark.

For imagining what Sister Loretta's hair might smell like when it's loose at night.

For dreaming about the courier's calloused fingers running over my ribs in a silence that isn't divine.

[He exhales—shaky, but steadier than before.]

If I am a vessel, then this is what I carry.

Heat and questions.

Shame and hunger.

The slow ache of a boy who isn't allowed to want but wants anyway.

[Click.]

Cassette G

[Click.]

[Church bells ring faintly in the background. Distant voices echo, laughing and joyful. Plates clatter. Music hums beneath it all. Then— Errevale's voice, quieter, more measured than usual.]

It's Feast Day.

Everyone's downstairs.

Candles. Banners. Bread in the shape of doves. Even Sister Mathilde sang.

They made me sit at the head table this year.

With a garland around my shoulders and a crown of rosemary on my head.

Like I was the offering, or something to be devoured.

[He breathes slowly—then chuckles, hollow.]

I suppose, in a way, I was.

They paraded me through the garden, then kissed my hands one by one like I was something holy.

Not someone.

[He speaks again, softer now. Distant, numb.]

I tried to smile.
Tried to mean it the way I used to.

But every time someone looked at me, I felt a little more transparent.
A little more made-up.

Like I wasn't celebrating with them. I was the celebration.
The idea of me.
The myth of Errevale.

[He shifts slightly. The sounds of laughter and music dim, like he's moved away from the celebration.]

They served honeyed wine. I didn't drink it.
I wanted to.
But I knew if I did, I might cry.
Or laugh too loud.
Or say something like: "I am not holy. I am just a boy with a good memory and a pretty face."

[He laughs quietly before sighing.]

And then what?

Would they crucify me in the garden?

Or worse, pretend they didn't hear me.

[He exhales, voice trembling just slightly.]

I don't want to be worshipped. Does God not say not to worship false idols?

[He pauses.]

In the Bible... the idols are always destroyed. God does not like them. So... perhaps God does not like me. Perhaps I will be destroyed.

[He sighs shakily, his fingers drumming on the desk.]

I don't want to be an idol.

I want someone to bring me a slice of cake and whisper "Happy Feast Day" like it's a shared joke, not a hymn.

I want to eat with my hands and laugh with my mouth open.

I want to be seen and not needed.

[Another pause. The bells ring again and he groans.]

I should go back before someone notices I'm gone.
They'll want to sing to me again.

[He snorts quietly.]

Don't smite me, God. I never asked for sainthood. But if you decide I deserve it, at least let me tell the procession to fuck off, just once.
[Click.]

[He laughs quietly before sighing.]

And then what?

Would they crucify me in the garden?

Or worse, pretend they didn't hear me.

[He exhales, voice trembling just slightly.]

I don't want to be worshipped. Does God not say not to worship false idols?

[He pauses.]

In the Bible... the idols are always destroyed. God does not like them. So… perhaps God does not like me. Perhaps I will be destroyed.

[He sighs shakily, his fingers drumming on the desk.]

I don't want to be an idol.

I want someone to bring me a slice of cake and whisper "Happy Feast Day" like it's a shared joke, not a hymn.

I want to eat with my hands and laugh with my mouth open.

I want to be seen and not needed.

[Another pause. The bells ring again and he groans.]

I should go back before someone notices I'm gone.
They'll want to sing to me again.

[He snorts quietly.]

Don't smite me, God. I never asked for sainthood. But if you decide I deserve it, at least let me tell the procession to fuck off, just once.

[Click.]

Je vous adresse mes sincères condoléances, Errevale...

Words From the Author

Well! This certainly was a ride!

From the bottom of my heart, thank you for picking up this book. I'm sure it's not perfect, there's so much more I'm sure I could have done better. But I'm quite proud of this!

I tend to write very sad characters, huh? For my second novel to be about another author who's life was brought to ruin by a story. I like to think Vattica, the main character from my debut novel *The Musings of He* would have felt for Errevale. Possible reminded him of his own brother. Maybe in another life, they could have saved one another from their manuscripts.

Alas! This is where Errevale's tale ends. On a rather sad note, maybe, but I think Callum did him justice.

While writing this, I initially planned to bring Benedict back as the editor. He's got a somewhat clinical outlook on the stories he edits. But I think Callum was the perfect editor for this. Someone who related to Errevale in a way, whether that be because they're close in age or because they both feel things quite deeply. I'm sure he's still thinking about the boy forced into sainthood. I'm sure he sometimes sneaks into the archives to listen to him laugh again.

I don't think he visits his grave, though. I'm sure he knows Errevale wouldn't like that. To be looked upon with sadness and a sense of pity. He's happier in a place where no one can see him, where no one can make him holy. He's happy to be forgotten in the quiet.

Admittedly, I worried about this subject a lot as someone that was raised a Christian. I hope I handled it delicately. I hope it wasn't disrespectful.

But I also feel like this is something a lot of people raised in religion, no matter what faith it is, can feel. The holiness.

The fear.

What it turns you into.

What it becomes.

Naturally this is a very ficticious and heightened version of it, but even so, I hope someone does feel it too.

Well! I'll end this here. Thank you again for reading, and I hope to see you in the next story.

Elowen Greywell
Head Curator & Archivist

Ink stains.
Memories linger.
Hillsather publishes both.